AT RISK

AT RISK

ALICE HOFFMAN

G. P. PUTNAM'S SONS / NEW YORK

The author gratefully acknowledges permission for the
use of lyrics from "True Blue" by Madonna Ciccone and
Stephen Bray, from the album *True Blue* copyright © 1986
by WB Music Corp., Blue Disque Company Inc., Webo Girl
Publishing, Black Lion Music (ASCAP). All U.S. and Canadian
rights controlled by the above publishers. All rights reserved.
Reprinted by permission of Madonna Ciccone and Stephen Bray.

This is a work of fiction. The events described are imaginary, and the
characters are fictitious and not intended to represent specific living persons.

The text of this book is set in Garamond.

Library of Congress Cataloging-in-Publication Data

Hoffman, Alice.
At risk / Alice Hoffman.
p.   cm.
I. Title.
ISBN 0-399-13367-4
PS3558.03447A86 1988   87-33240 CIP
813'.54—dc19

Printed in the United States of America
3   4   5   6   7   8   9   10

The author wishes to thank Tom Martin for untold kindnesses during the writing of this book. She would also like to thank the members of her writers' group for their continuing support; Perri Klass for her generous and careful reading of the manuscript; the late Joseph Savago for his advocacy and his invaluable comments; and Faith Sale for her encouragement and her friendship.

AT RISK

I

THERE IS A WASP in the kitchen. Drawn by the smell of apricot jam, lazy from the morning's heat, the wasp hovers above the children. All through town a yellow light is cast over the green lawns and the rhododendrons. By dusk there will be a storm, with raindrops that are surprisingly cold, but of course by then the birds in the backyards and out on the marsh will have taken flight. Where do birds go in the rain? How do they disappear so thoroughly? Already, the sparrows in the chestnut tree are restless. They're not fooled by the pure yellow light any more than they're fooled by this last burst of August heat.

"Look at her abdomen," Charlie says of the wasp. "It's full of eggs."

Amanda, who at eleven is older than her brother by three years, puts a dish towel over her head. "Get it out of here!" she says. "Kill it now, and I mean it."

"No way," Charlie says. He is a collector of specimens, a lover of anything mildly revolting: frogs, insects in bottles, bats' wings, centipedes. "I don't have to take orders from someone who still wears braces," Charlie informs his sister.

"Mom," Amanda yells.

The wasp, startled, flees to the ceiling.

"Oh, great," Charlie moans. He stands up on his chair and lifts the jam jar into the air to tempt the wasp from her hiding place.

"You are really disgusting," Amanda tells Charlie. "Mom!" she yells.

"Chicken," Charlie says to his sister.

"Moron," Amanda counters.

Their mother, Polly Farrell, who is out in the garden, can hear the children arguing. It's been hard, but she has trained herself to tune out their squabbles; otherwise she'd spend most of her time refereeing. She never pays her garden much attention either, but this year the voles obviously found the small untended patch fascinating. In the hardware section of the corner store, Jack Larson told her to bury sticks of dynamite under her vegetables, and the smell of sulfur would scare away the voles. But the idea of her vegetables resting on explosives made Polly too uncomfortable. Instead, she stuck blue-tipped kitchen matches around each plant. Needless to say, whole stalks of broccoli and all of her carrots and lettuce have disappeared underground. The only thing the voles wouldn't touch were the zucchini, and they've gone berserk. Polly has been putting zucchini into everything, and by now her children can ferret it out no matter how well she disguises it. Last night she deep-fried it and tried to pass it off as onion rings, but Charlie immediately removed the doughy breading and unmasked the zucchini. Amanda has taken a recent vow not to eat anything green.

Polly snaps off two large zucchini and hides them under her white cotton shirt. Tonight she plans to chop the zucchini up and sneak it into the meatloaf. She has to do something. Thin green tendrils are climbing up the chicken-wire fence around the garden, and even her husband, Ivan, who'll eat just about anything, buttered, burned, or stale, is starting to complain and search through the freezer for packages of French beans and mixed Italian vegetables. Before she opens the screen door, Polly wipes her hands on her faded blue jeans; as soon as she's inside, she ducks into the pantry and hides the zucchini she's picked behind a row of cereal boxes.

"Mom, this is really serious," Amanda calls. "I really mean it."

Polly straightens her shirt and comes into the kitchen. She pulls the dish towel off Amanda's head so that her daughter's blond hair stands straight up from her scalp in pale, spokelike strands. Polly quickly feels Amanda's forehead. Amanda has been dragging around a summer cold since June and, although she insists her throat no longer hurts, her forehead is still warm.

"I want you to take some Tylenol," Polly says. "Now."

"Charlie has a wasp in here," Amanda says.

Polly looks up at the ceiling. "Charlie!" she says. She pulls Charlie down from the chair.

"I didn't bring her in the house," Charlie insists. "She flew in all by herself. And anyway," he tells his sister, "she has as much right to live here as you do."

Polly, who's allergic to bee stings, steps toward the doorway just in case the wasp shoots down toward her.

"Ivan," she calls. "A wasp!"

"A what?" Ivan calls back.

Amanda and Charlie look at each other and try not to laugh; it's their mother's main complaint, their father hears only what he wants to hear.

"Very funny," Polly says to the children. "A wasp," she shouts.

"A female," Charlie yells. "She's got about a zillion eggs in her abdomen." Charlie then looks at his mother apologetically. "That ought to get him in here," he explains.

Ivan comes into the kitchen and shoos them all out. He's tall, with that posture reserved for tall men; he resembles a stork when he runs. To Polly, Ivan still looks as young as he did when they met, though he was thirty-eight last March. No matter how annoyed she is with him, and she's often annoyed, particularly because Ivan has grown more forgetful and in some odd way less involved with her, Polly still loves the way he looks, more so because she knows Ivan never gives his appearance a second thought. He's happiest wearing frayed sweaters and unwashed chinos; he'd never have his hair cut if Polly didn't remind him.

"Your hero approaches the wasp," Ivan says.

"Oh, yeah!" the children shout gleefully from the hallway.

"Right above you!" Polly says.

The children peer into the kitchen and giggle as their father grabs a colander from the counter and puts it over his head.

"Protective measures," Ivan calls through the holes in the colander.

After he opens the windows and the back door, Ivan rolls up a newspaper then gets onto a chair. He waves the newspaper at the wasp, but Polly can tell he's not really aiming at the damned thing. He doesn't want to hurt it.

"Ivan," Polly says coldly. At this moment he is hardly her hero. "Just kill it."

Ivan removes the colander from his head so he can look at her. He has to crouch so he won't hit the ceiling.

"You want to try?" he suggests.

"Do it your way," Polly says, and she leaves the children there to watch Ivan gently coax the wasp out an open window while she goes off to hunt for her car keys.

It's a good thing August is almost over. They have had all summer together and are long past the point of getting on each other's nerves. There's been a mood of dissatisfaction in the house; the days have been too hot and too long, there's been too much time left open for arguments. Ivan, who's an astronomer, usually divides his time between his own research and teaching a graduate seminar at the institute he helped to found. This summer he's had no classes and has been working on a paper he will present at a conference in Florida in a few weeks. Ivan is not pleased with the paper, which he's been aimlessly rewriting, or with the fact that he has been scheduled as one of the last speakers, at an hour so late that most of the other astronomers will have already left the state. Polly is no happier with her work. She feels vaguely embarrassed by it and has kept it a secret from people like her parents, who she knows would disapprove. She's involved in what the children have dubbed the Casper Project: photographing the séances of a local medium, working with Betsy Stafford, an author whose books her photographs have illustrated twice before. But Charlie is the most discontented of all. He's spent the past two months perfecting his obnoxious behavior with too much TV and with collecting a basementful of specimens, including some field mice Polly can hear squeaking at night. Charlie complains that his parents favor Amanda and treat him like a baby; the only person he can stand to be with is his best friend, Sevrin, Betsy Stafford's son. But whenever the boys are together, and they're together night and day, they do something irresponsible—track a skunk through the woods or bike through heavy traffic to the mall—which only proves Ivan and Polly right when they refuse Charlie privileges.

Amanda is the only one with any real purpose this summer. She has dedicated herself to gymnastics and has gone from the self-conscious beginner she was last year to one of the best students in the gymnastics camp the elementary school has been running this summer. Amanda cannot walk through a parking lot without balancing on the raised yellow dividers; the swing hanging from the willow tree in the yard has been replaced by a wooden bar. It still amazes Polly that this girl who can throw herself onto the uneven parallel bars with a grace that is almost like flight is her daughter. Somehow, while Polly wasn't looking, Amanda became her own person. When she watches her daughter compete, Polly feels what Laurel Smith, the medium she has been photographing, calls the "cold hand," a piercing physical reaction to something extraordinary. At those times Amanda is not the child Polly covers at night with an extra quilt, the girl who leaves her leotards on the floor, who has to be cajoled into going to the orthodontist. She is a creature Polly cannot name, one made up not of flesh but of points of brilliant light.

"You'd rather have Daddy get stung than kill that stupid wasp," Amanda says to Charlie after the wasp has been directed out the window and car keys and backpacks and gym bags have all been collected.

Amanda looks over at Ivan, concerned. It's a look Polly has been noticing a lot more often lately. Suddenly, Amanda is interested in how Ivan feels and what he thinks. When he talks, Amanda listens. When Polly talks, Amanda puts on her Walkman. And, Polly knows, it's only the beginning. By the time Amanda is fourteen, Polly will be lucky if her daughter speaks to her, never mind listens to her. Polly remembers only too well when she cut off her own mother, Claire. In her memory still, it's as if she had two mothers: the warm person she loved to touch and be near and the weak, disappointing creature she realized her mother was as soon as Polly turned thirteen. Of course, circumstances were different. Claire had already disappointed Polly, but Polly has never wavered from her adolescent assessment of Claire, and now that worries her. Amanda was an easy child, the kind who edges onto your lap, who never had to be told to hold hands when crossing the street. Sooner or later, she'll have to hate her mother, and all Polly can hope for is that their break will be temporary, that it won't cause any permanent damage.

While Ivan guides the children out the back door, Polly taps down the broken porch step with the heel of her shoe. The house is white, with black shutters; the porch ceiling is a soft blue, as though a wedge of the noonday sky had been caught inside the wood. With its oval windows on the stair landings and its wide, sloping floorboards, it's the kind of house Polly always dreamed of having as a child. But Charlie and Amanda take it for granted and treat it badly. They slam doors and complain about drafts; their idea of a great house is something modern and sleek, with skylights and lofts and cable TV.

"You really make me sick," Amanda tells her brother.

"Thank you," Charlie says, with a formal bow.

Originally, Polly and Ivan moved up to Cape Ann from Boston for the children. But, as it turns out, they're the ones who have become most attached. It's not only the house they fell in love with but the town. Morrow has a wicked history, one the children have no interest in, a history prettily disguised by the large white sea captains' houses, and the town common ringed with shops, and the day-trippers up from Boston all summer, here for the wide, smooth beaches. Whether or not two witches were drowned in the pond in the center of the common is uncertain, but many towns in Massachusetts could claim that heritage. What nearly turned Morrow into a ghost town was the influenza epidemic after World War I. Whole families perished in single rooms. Children were lost one after another, wives locked themselves in attics so they would not infect their husbands. For years afterward no one was interested in the sea captains' houses or the summer cottages, even though the reason they were abandoned was long forgotten. In the sixties newcomers from Boston who knew nothing of the epidemic began to buy up houses, cheap, and some of the vegetarian restaurants and craft shops they opened are still in operation, though their prices are much higher now. The school superintendent began to hire Harvard graduates, who, in a later era, might have gone on to business or law school, but who, in 1965, were drawn to a small town where their dogs could run free and summers could be spent digging clams and getting suntans. By the time Polly and Ivan were looking for a house, Morrow's school district had been rated among the top ten in the Commonwealth. That alone was reason to move.

Of course, the children tell them often enough how they plan to leave town as soon as they turn eighteen. Amanda wants to live in Manhattan. Charlie alternates between Alaska and California.

"Good. Go. I'll pay for your plane fare," Ivan tells them during arguments when they taunt him with how much distance they intend to put between themselves and their parents once they're free to do as they please. But when the children are in bed, and Polly and Ivan sit out on the porch and watch lightning bugs drift through the bushes, they find themselves wishing they could stop time and keep Amanda and Charlie children forever.

Impossible, and yet they hope.

"No Laurel Smith today?" Ivan teases Polly as she gets the kids into the Blazer.

"Don't make fun of Laurel," Polly tells Ivan. She leans on the open door of the Blazer, only now remembering she has an appointment to take it in for new shocks this afternoon.

"I knew it!" Ivan says. "You're falling for her garbage. You're so suggestible."

"I am not," Polly says.

This summer, Polly had her long, dark hair cut into short layers with the idea of facing up to her thirty-sixth birthday, but instead of making her look her age, the new haircut has her looking as young as a graduate student.

"I suggest we send them off in a cab and go back to bed," Ivan whispers.

Polly grins at him, not taking his proposal seriously.

"You make time for Laurel Smith," Ivan complains.

"That's work," Polly says, annoyed.

"Mom," Amanda calls from the backseat, "I don't want to be the last one there."

"She doesn't want to be the last one there," Polly tells Ivan, grateful for a way out of a conversation which, she knows, will end with Ivan accusing her of what he himself is guilty of: too many hours spent working.

"A fate worse than death," Ivan says. He kisses Polly and Polly kisses him back. Before Ivan moves away, she quickly bites his lip.

"That's for being mean about my job," Polly says as she gets into the car.

"I was not mean," Ivan insists. He leans in the window and kisses Amanda, walks around the Blazer toward the ancient Karmann-Ghia he refuses to give up, then leans into Charlie's window. "It's just that I'm medium cool about Laurel Smith," he puns, and the children both let out a groan.

"Dad, that was pathetic," Charlie says.

"Let me out of here," Ivan says. "I'm going where I'm appreciated."

"Oh, yeah?" Polly grins, knowing how unappreciated Ivan has been feeling lately. "Where's that?"

"Mother, do you have to argue?" Amanda says from the backseat.

Ivan and Polly stare at each other. One of them is amused; the other isn't.

"Don't gloat," Polly tells Ivan. "You'll be the one they turn on next."

Ivan grins and gets into his car. He waves as he backs out of the driveway, and after he's gone Polly reaches for her sunglasses and heads for the Cheshire School. Charlie sits glumly beside her; as always, he is going with them against his will. As far as he's concerned, anyone who isn't his best friend, Sevrin, is just a pain in the neck. As she's backing down the driveway, Polly gets a glimpse of Amanda's thoughtful, unreadable face in the rearview mirror. Amanda is always distant before a meet; her nervousness takes the form of an unearthly calm so that Polly has to say everything to her twice before Amanda hears her.

There's a séance today, which Polly is missing, but it's worth it. She has been photographing séances—what Laurel Smith calls readings—since June, and so far not one spirit has appeared on film. Polly has tried slower shutter speeds and faster film, she has switched from color to black-and-white. Some of the photographs, though ghost free, are remarkable. In several Laurel Smith, who is a few years younger than Polly, is completely unrecognizable. There's a photograph in which she looks like an old, dark woman and another in which she doesn't appear to be more than a child, with her heavy, pale hair fanned out behind her as though dripping with water. The one photograph Polly has found herself going back to again and again was taken during a reading in which Laurel had contacted a client's husband who was killed in a car crash. Without a doubt, in that photograph, there is a scar along Laurel Smith's forehead.

"Either she's a great actress," Polly once told Betsy Stafford, "or something real is going on here."

Betsy, who is much more of a cynic than Polly, had smiled and said, "You'll have to wait and read the book to find out the answer." Even after she'd seen some of the photographs, Betsy had refused to admit that Laurel might be anything but a charlatan.

"Let's just accept Laurel for what she is," Betsy insisted. "A nut."

Polly will always be grateful to Betsy because Betsy is the one who pulled Polly out of her indecision about whether or not to become a professional, an act for which there will never be enough thanks. Their first collaboration—an activity book for preschoolers—was begun after the two women met through their sons, both in the same nursery school. Charlie and Sevrin have remained best friends, yet the relationship between their mothers remains professional by choice, even though Polly knows, via Charlie, all sorts of odd and intimate details about Betsy's life she might otherwise not know: That she allows the sugary breakfast cereals Polly frowns on. That Betsy's husband, Frank, an attorney who commutes into Boston, often does not get home until past nine and when he and Betsy fight they don't bother to close the bedroom door. They curse when they fight, loudly. Charlie's told her so.

Polly admits to being the passive partner. Betsy is the one who writes the proposals, then goes out and gets the book contracts, and afterward hires Polly. So perhaps it is not a partnership at all, except that it feels like one. Particularly since their last book, an in-depth study of coping with death, is a choice Polly herself would have never made. She almost turned down the project, but the fee was too seductive, enough to pay for gymnastics camp and orthodontists and hamster cages for years to come. After photographing her first terminal patient, Polly spent half an hour throwing up by the side of the road. It never got easier, whether the sessions were in a hospital, a hospice, or the subject's home. Only two of the people she photographed have not yet died, an elderly woman with cancer and a young man in Boston with an inoperable tumor at the base of his skull. Both write to Polly occasionally, and she always writes back, but she never looks at the finished book, though it is the project that allowed her to say no, now and forever, to photographing birthday parties and weddings.

The book about Laurel Smith was supposed to cheer them up. A lighter book, it was to be a mild debunking. It has not turned out that way. Laurel looks more like a librarian than a medium and, séances aside, her behavior is extremely sensible. She has long blond hair like Amanda's, and deep-set gray eyes. She never bothers with makeup, and Polly has never seen her wear any jewelry other than two rings, one a small pearl set in gold, the other a thin silver band. Though her clients seem willing to pay any amount necessary to reach the spirits they long to contact, Laurel never changes her fee. No matter how rich her client, she always charges two hundred dollars for a reading. Betsy, who unbeknownst to Laurel has been researching her background and discovered a small trust fund left to Laurel by her parents, doesn't give Laurel any credit for generosity. But Polly is not so quick to judge her. There have been times, inside Laurel's cottage, when Polly has found herself believing in an afterlife. She tells herself it is the powerful conviction of Laurel's clients, all so desperately convinced whoever they have loved and lost can be reached, that affects her. Or it is the place itself, the movement of reeds and cattails in the marsh, the way the light falls and is caught inside the pearl Laurel wears on her finger.

By the time Polly drives into the parking lot at the elementary school, the heat has begun to drift up from the asphalt in snaky waves. The glass windows along the gym look smoky and dark, making the place seem empty, but it's just an illusion. The windows have been treated to keep out the sun; on the other side of the glass, the gym is already filling up with parents. Polly knows she can't stop Amanda from becoming a teenager, but she's thankful that the combined high school and junior high is on the other side of town, so that Amanda will be protected from mixing with high school students for another year.

Amanda gets out of the car, carrying her pink nylon gym bag like a professional, slinging it over her arm, hardly noticing its weight. Strands of her hair have slipped out of the elastic band that holds her ponytail. This is the last meet of the summer, and Amanda is excited about her best three events: floor exercise, the balance beam, and vaulting. In her bag she has her cassette ready, Duran Duran's "Hungry Like the Wolf." Amanda is sweating too much; the heat is bothering her, or maybe she's more nervous than she'd thought. When she woke up this morning her sheets were drenched with sweat. She wants to win this meet. She doesn't mention the Olympics anymore because people like her parents get sappy, patronizing looks on their faces when she does. She knows hundreds of other girls dream of going to Texas and having Bela Karolyi as their coach, but Amanda is actually saving her money. All she wants is one audition. If he tells her she's not good enough, she'll have to accept it.

Of course the truth is, she can't imagine him telling her that.

"Knock them dead," Polly tells her when they reach the door to the school. She hugs Amanda tightly, and when Amanda runs off to the locker room, Polly and Charlie head over to the gym. Charlie continues to read as he walks up the bleachers; it drives Polly crazy that he doesn't watch where he's going, but she bites her tongue. She's learned to save her reprimands, to dole them out carefully, in the hopes that they might actually count for something.

When they find a place in the bleachers, Charlie takes off his backpack and sits down, then unzips the backpack and gets out another dinosaur book. He is a *Tyrannosaurus rex* devotee. He can tell you how long a tyrannosaurus's teeth measured and exactly where paleontologists have gathered his remains. Charlie is a lot like his father was at that age. Ivan always says that the sure sign of a budding scientist is that he carries books everywhere he goes so he won't have to be bored by people.

"Polly, I'm hearing strange things about you."

It is Evelyn Crowley's mother, Fran. The Crowleys live across the street from the Farrells, and Evelyn is one of Cheshire's top competitors, especially in the uneven parallel bars, around which she throws her small body with a vengeance. Fran sits down next to Polly. "The occult?" Fran says.

Outside, the temperature hovers around ninety, but here in the gym it's at least five degrees hotter, and the competition hasn't even started. Polly hopes Fran will think her face is flushed with heat, not embarrassment.

"If you mean I'm photographing Laurel Smith, you're right," Polly says, more coolly than she means to. "It's pretty darned occult," she adds with a laugh.

"I wish I had had the sort of dedication these girls have when I was young," Fran says as the locker-room doors are swung open.

"Maybe they're just stupid," Charlie says without looking up from his book.

Polly and Fran have been friends for years—which is probably why Amanda and Evelyn can't stand each other—but Polly doesn't mind that Charlie has insulted her, she isn't even bothered by the fact that Charlie is clearly more interested in extinct reptiles than in his sister's success. The girls have begun to file in from the locker room, and Polly can't help it, she's nervous. There are fifteen gymnasts from Amanda's program, another fifteen from a school in Gloucester. In their leotards, the girls seem awkward and uncomfortable as the onlookers cheer. Amanda is easy to spot because she is the blondest and, at five feet two, one of the tallest. Some of the girls smile when they spy a parent in the audience, but Amanda, always conscious of her braces, keeps her mouth firmly closed. Polly knows Amanda hopes she won't grow any more; the smaller the gymnast is, the better her chances of staying in the sport. Amanda is second in line to vault the horse and she does so easily, with real power and grace. Polly claps her hands so hard they hurt.

"Don't embarrass her, Mom," Charlie tells her.

Amanda is less sure of herself on the uneven parallel bars, but certainly she's better than most. One poor girl falls at the very start of her routine, and she falls hard, turning one of her ankles so badly she can't continue. Even Charlie looks up when she lurches out of the gym in tears. Polly is thankful that it's somebody else's daughter who's fallen and not hers, and then is disturbed by how much she feels like a stage mother. She realizes that her fists are clenched. A square of sunlight from the highest window in the gym settles on the polished wooden floor. Polly unclenches her fists when Amanda finishes her routine on the balance beam. She has gotten the highest score so far, but afterward Amanda sits down near a pile of mats and the coach kneels down beside her. Polly worries that something is wrong, but soon Amanda gets up and goes over to her team, where she waits for her last event, her best: floor exercise.

"Our girls are terrific," Fran says to Polly. And Polly agrees. If she were the judge she'd be hard-pressed to decide between the two. Perhaps that's why it's possible for her and Fran to sit together at meets. All along the bleachers other mothers, and a few fathers, are intent on watching only their own daughters.

Charlie's knees are pulled up to form a table and his book lies open upon them. His hair, cut short, is damp with sweat. Polly thinks she recognizes a drawing of a hadrosaurus. She knows most of the dinosaurs by now, knows which were fierce carnivores

25

and which ate only marsh plants. She would like to put her arm around Charlie, but, knowing he would be mortified, instead rests her hand against his knee. Charlie looks up at her, misreading her cue, ready to leave. Then they both hear the first beats of "Hungry Like the Wolf." Charlie makes a face.

"Can't you put that book away?" Polly whispers.

"No," Charlie says, "I can't."

He has read this book dozens of times and is no less interested than he was the first time through. Sometimes his lips move when he reads, and Polly knows he is memorizing facts. When she looks at him, Polly often gets a vision of him as a toddler, solemnly counting stones or beads, content to watch a spider build her web, his nature already so set that his first word, spoken at a pond, was not "mama" or "dada" but "quack."

Amanda begins her routine with a roundoff, two back hand-springs, and a backflip. Polly, who swims, but is otherwise not athletic, feels that spooky, cold sensation along the back of her neck. Amanda's feet barely touch the mat. She does a forward roll, then a handstand and full pirouette. There is some scattered applause. The girls on the other team are watching her carefully; it's a terrific performance and everyone knows it. Polly's eyes feel hot. When Amanda is through she bows, beautifully. Polly doesn't give a damn whom she'll embarrass, she gets to her feet and applauds.

"Not bad," Charlie admits grudgingly when Polly sits back down.

Polly grins and gives him a shove. When Amanda is announced as the highest scorer, Polly stands again and applauds. Other parents are standing up on the bleachers below her and Polly has to strain to see Amanda, who's so composed you'd never guess she had won. Amanda bows, then quickly leaves the floor, as though now that the scoring is over, she has no interest in the gym.

"She deserved to win," Evelyn's mother tells Polly.

"They were all great," Polly says, with more generosity than she feels.

Polly aims Charlie toward the door and tells him she'll meet him out by the car. She greets several parents she knows on the floor, then stops to shake the coach's hand.

"I can tell you've been working them hard, Jack," Polly says.

"You should be proud of her," Jack Eagan tells her.

"I am," Polly says, delighted that at last there is someone with whom she doesn't have to play down her excitement.

"She picked herself right up after that bad start," the coach says.

Polly, who didn't notice a bad start, smiles and heads for the lockers. Tonight they will take Amanda out to dinner to celebrate, maybe to Dexter's, which has great fried clams and fries. Polly will sneak a call to Ivan so he can stop on the way home and buy flowers; after all her hard work, Amanda deserves to be treated like a champion.

The locker room smells musty and lockers are clanging. Here the gymnasts look more like the little girls they are. One, when she sees Polly, quickly covers her bare, undeveloped chest. Polly walks along the aisles, looking for Amanda. Instead, she sees Evelyn Crowley.

"You had some great routines," she tells Evelyn.

Evelyn smiles, but Polly can see her disappointment.

"I didn't practice enough," Evelyn says.

"Have you seen Amanda?" Polly asks.

Evelyn shrugs. Amanda is probably the last person she wants to see right now.

"Maybe she's in the showers," Evelyn says.

Polly walks toward the rear of the locker room. She sees Amanda's unzipped gym bag hanging in an open locker. Inside there are barrettes and a hairbrush and a necklace made out of tiny

27

plastic beads that look like seed pearls, which Amanda sometimes wears before a meet for good luck.

The showers are all turned on and Polly can hear the voices of the little girls, a murmur that can just as easily explode into giggles or a contemptuous rating of someone's routine. Polly has decided, they will definitely have fried clams tonight. When they go home they'll sit out on the porch to watch for the last few lightning bugs. They'll hear a chorus of frogs, both from the marshy inlets that surround Morrow and from the aquarium inside the house where Charlie is temporarily keeping a bullfrog, which he swears is the last of the specimens he'll bring home, just as he swears it's a matter of life and death for him to record the number of croaks per hour during various weather conditions. Maybe Polly can persuade Amanda to give up one day's practice and go to the beach with her tomorrow, just the two of them. When they were little, it was hard for Polly to divide her time equally between the children. Charlie and Amanda wanted such different things that one of them always had to be put on hold, and either way Polly felt torn between them. No matter what she did, she always had the nagging sense she was disappointing someone. But now things have changed; the children prefer to be with their friends and Polly has to wheedle hours for herself. Polly often thinks about this when her mother calls from New York, but it never stops her from cutting the conversation short, from always being the first to hang up.

The closer Polly gets to the showers, the stronger the smell of ammonia. They use some awful heavy-duty cleaner and the result is dizzying.

"Hi, Polly," a high voice says, and Polly turns and hugs Amanda's best friend, Jessie Eagan, who is also the daughter of the coach. Jessie is a good gymnast, but she's not passionate the way Amanda is, and maybe that's why she can cheer for Amanda and feel no jealousy. It's too bad Jessie's not serious, because she has a perfect gymnast's body, she's only four feet six and amazingly light. She has brown hair, cut short, and golden eyes. Both she and Amanda are in love with some singer in a rock group, whom they refer to by his first name, Brian, as though they were on intimate terms with him.

"Amanda was fantastic," Jessie says. "Even my dad says so."

Clearly, the coach is not one to hand out compliments.

"Come out to dinner with us tonight," Polly says.

"I can't," Jessie says mournfully. "Don't tell me if you're going to go out for clams because I'll be trapped at my aunt's having something gross."

Polly hugs Jessie again and walks on toward the showers. She forces herself not to laugh when she sees one of the girls showering with her bra on, and in fact she's a little shocked that an eleven- or twelve-year-old would even wear a bra. The sound of the showers makes it seem as though the room were under water. The tiles are green, and there are no windows back here. Polly sees a hand from inside one of the showers holding onto the outside wall. Without thinking, she begins to run.

Amanda is doubled over; her blond hair looks green. She is vomiting in the shower, her whole body heaving. A towel she had tried to wrap around herself has fallen to the floor and is soaked. The water is still running. Polly feels absolutely cold. Maybe it's all this water, the tiles, the green tint of the fluorescent lights. She puts her hands on Amanda's shoulders and tries to support her. Amanda doesn't seem to notice that her mother is there. She keeps vomiting until she has nothing to throw up but yellow bile. When Amanda stops vomiting, she's so weak Polly has trouble holding her up.

"You'll be okay," Polly says.

"I don't feel good," Amanda tells her.

Too much excitement, Polly thinks. Too much pressure. She puts her palm against Amanda's forehead and realizes that her daughter has a fever, a high one. Polly reaches the taps and turns off the hot, then cups her hand so she can scoop cold water over Amanda's face. They are facing each other, with Amanda leaning against her so that Polly is soaked through her clothes.

"I'm freezing," Amanda says.

In fact she is hotter than before.

Polly drags Amanda out of the shower, sits her on a bench, then grabs a towel and wraps it around her. She runs to the locker, gets the pink gym bag, then runs back and quickly begins to dress her daughter. Amanda feels heavy, as limp as straw.

"Ow," Amanda says as Polly maneuvers one leg into a pair of shorts.

Polly gently touches the back of Amanda's knee and feels that the joint is swollen. She finishes dressing Amanda and helps her to stand.

"You'll be better in the morning," Polly says.

It's what she always says when the children are sick, and they always believe her. But this time Polly is wrong. Just after dusk the rain will begin, but it won't bring any relief. In the morning, the last day of August and the hottest on record, Amanda will still be shivering beneath two cotton quilts.

2

LAUREL SMITH loves coffee and cream. It is her weakness. Just the smell of it makes her lick her lips like a cat. She pours a second cup from the glass coffeepot into a yellow mug, a cheap piece of pottery with just the right-size handle. It's low tide and egrets out in the marsh are closer to her cottage than usual. There are no screens on the windows, but when Laurel has her coffee she always pushes the windows open so she can listen to the birds, even though it means later she will suffer the bites of mosquitoes who manage to get inside.

She has forgotten to feed the cat, Stella. Although Stella is black, she's hardly a familiar. A familiar should be utterly feline and Stella is more like a dog. She will retrieve a ball if you throw one for her; she follows along on walks; she doesn't mind the water and has been known to jump into the marsh, after a duck or Canada goose twice her size. Laurel goes to the pantry for a pack of Tender Vittles and Stella follows, rubbing against Laurel's white kimono. Outside, it's brutally hot, but the cottage is backed by tall pine trees that always keep it cool; not a plus in November or in the heart of February, but today the linoleum against Laurel's bare feet is wonderfully cold. As long as she's up, Laurel gets an egg, fills a blue tin pot with water, and sets it to boil. She had a husband once who said she could not even boil an egg. Clearly he was wrong.

He was wrong about a lot of things. Laurel never tricked him into marrying her. He fell in love with her all on his own; he chose to ignore how shy she was, how ill at ease with people, including, it's true, himself. He accused her of so many things, Laurel can no longer remember the list, although she certainly remembers how often he insisted that she was in love with death. He was more wrong about this than anything else; Laurel is, and always has been, terrified by death. When a baby cries, she hears a death rattle. The branches of a white birch are crossbones. She cannot look at spaded earth, even if it is only a corner of a suburban lawn dug up for a new rhododendron.

She never wanted to receive messages, it just started to happen to her when she was twelve, beginning with what she thought was a dream. She was walking down a long corridor, which became more narrow as she went along, the walls and ceiling curving until the corridor became a tunnel. She stopped. Everything around her was cold. In the distance she could see her grandmother falling. Laurel's grandmother wore a blue silk dress and a long rope of pearls, and she was falling downward, as though the tunnel were vertical, straight down from sky to earth. There was no pull of gravity, so every path was a slow circular spiral.

In the morning the call came that Laurel's grandmother was dead. She had been at a wedding and had fallen; she'd had a stroke and never regained consciousness. Laurel received several other messages from her grandmother; she was terrified, but she told no one. The messages that came through her dreams grew more and more specific, as if someone were trying to prove something to her. She dreamed her grandmother was winding the chiming clock in her kitchen, and the following day the clock arrived, airmail. She dreamed her grandmother led her to an angel with his wings folded tightly against his body, and when her parents took her to the cemetery there was the angel, carved into her grandmother's headstone.

When she was thirteen, the messages began to come to her during her waking hours, messages from people she had never known in life. She could close her eyes in math class and hear a child's voice, a classmate's sister lost at birth. She dreaded the cold, clammy way her hands felt whenever she was near someone who had suffered a recent loss. While other girls her age were thinking about shades of lipstick and Saturday nights, Laurel could not stop thinking about the brevity of a human lifespan. At night her dreams were terrifying things filled with cemeteries, silence, full white moons.

When she was seventeen Laurel made a huge effort, and, with the help of a prescription for Valium, she nearly succeeded and stopped thinking about death. She finished high school, went to college, married when she was twenty-two. For a while her husband didn't mind her odd habits. He overlooked it when she hid in closets during thunderstorms, when she refused to leave the house for three weeks after their cat was run over by a car, when she couldn't accompany him to his father's funeral. It was true, he had plenty to complain about, everything she did she did halfheartedly. She'd start the laundry but never finish, so that her husband wore damp clothes to work. The frozen dinners she cooked were always icy in the middle. She was still receiving messages, but they were jumbled now, as though she had a crossed connection, and she had a constant, dull headache. What Laurel could never understand was why, when he started to notice and list her faults, her husband seemed so surprised.

After her divorce, she moved to the cottage in Morrow and began to give readings. At first the messages came through with piercing clarity, but lately she's found herself drifting and she's taken to lying. It's easy; her clients give themselves away in a thousand ways. All she has to do is pick up on their clues, listen for their breathing to quicken, see if they've been biting nails. She has a new client today, at eleven. It's a bad time of day for a reading, dusk is better, or at least late afternoon, but this client's husband disapproves of séances and he'll be home from his golf game by two.

Laurel makes the bed, showers, and dresses in a white shirt and a denim wrap-around skirt. She brushes her long hair, her one vanity, just as coffee is her one vice. In her bookcase there are mostly cookbooks and novels, and, hidden in the back, some detective stories. Nothing about the occult. Laurel avoids psychic gatherings; she cringes when she reads about channelers who hold public meetings with audiences of hundreds of followers. There are no candles in her cottage, no crystal balls or baskets of herbs. The furniture is mostly wicker and oak collected at auctions and secondhand stores. Her newest, most prized acquisition is a tall brass lamp that has a pink silk shade. She paid too much for it. She had planned to keep it beside the window, behind the wicker couch, but when she got the lamp home Laurel hid it in a dark corner in her bedroom. She didn't understand why she'd done this until the photographer who's been coming around spotted the lamp. Polly found it so charming that she wanted the lamp included in any photographs she took and asked if it could be moved beside the table where Laurel did her readings. Laurel had insisted that the lamp would be too distracting. She had realized, all at once, that she should never have bought it. Pink silk and death did not go together.

It is the last day of August, and the last day of any month

depresses Laurel. She remembers now that she dreamed about her childhood, and she never dreams anymore. Her sleep is usually empty and deep, as if she used up all her dream time during her waking hours. In less than an hour, Betsy, whom Laurel always thinks of as "Bossy" ever since she managed to talk Laurel into being the subject for her book, will arrive with the photographer. Stupidly, Laurel has forgotten to mention the presence of a writer and a photographer to her new client, who is so nervous and secretive she may bolt and run as soon as she sees a camera. It will be hard enough to concentrate on a reading in this heat.

Outside, the sunlight is thick, like a swarm of yellow bees. It used to be easy for Laurel to resist sunlight like this; she doesn't even think she noticed sunlight before she moved here to the marsh. She cracks the brown shell of the hard-boiled egg she has on her counter, then eats standing up. She's edgy; something's not right. Laurel goes to let the cat out; then for no reason she follows Stella out onto the wooden deck. The deck, which juts out from the house, is built on stilts right over the marsh. At night, Laurel can hear crabs clattering in through holes, burrowing in the damp basement, which is often flooded at high tide when there's a full moon. Once, she found a starfish on the cellar stairs. She leans on the railing and feels the sun through her cotton blouse and on her bare legs. Before she came here, Laurel Smith had never seen a kingfisher; she couldn't tell the difference between a cardinal and a wren. In a few minutes Betsy Stafford and the new client will both pull into the dirt driveway, but Polly will not be coming to photograph the reading. It doesn't matter, there will be nothing to photograph and Laurel Smith knows it. She feels a pressure on her forehead, like a hand pushing against her.

Out on the marsh, two egrets take flight, struggling furiously for distance, as if frightened for their lives.

3

CHARLIE MAKES himself French toast. He leaves the eggy bowl on the counter and the burned frying pan on the stove. Summer is so boring, but he dreads the thought of school. Ten more days of freedom. Today he and Sevrin are going to sneak down to the pond, which both their mothers think is too far for them to bicycle to, and look for specimens. They have a theory that not only can sugar not harm you, it is actually good for you, and they intend to set up an experiment that will prove them right, down in Sevrin's basement, where no one ever goes. Charlie's backpack is bulging with the Mason jars he's pilfered from the pantry. He hopes his mother won't notice they're missing until next June, when she wants to make strawberry jam. Maybe, when the experiment has been completed, Charlie can set the newts free and replace the Mason jars so that his mother will never know anything amphibian was ever in them. He makes himself laugh thinking about what his mother could find on the shelf: strawberry jam, orange newt, pickled cucumbers, little green frogs in vinegar.

If Charlie catches whatever his sister has, and misses out on this last week of freedom, he will commit hara-kiri. He has a million things to do in ten days. The door slams as Charlie is pouring syrup on his French toast. Ivan has already been to the drugstore before setting out for the institute.

"Hey, buddy," Ivan says to Charlie. He eyes the French toast. "Looks good."

Polly comes down from upstairs. She's been sponging Amanda down with cool water, just as the doctor told her to do when she phoned during the call-in hour.

"Did you get the Tylenol and the Gatorade?" she asks Ivan.

Ivan produces the Tylenol. "No Gatorade at Larson's," he says.

"That's all you tried?" Polly says, furious. "One damn store?"

Charlie feels bad for his father; he tends to forget things, too, especially when he runs errands.

"I'll go back out," Ivan says.

Polly knows he is supposed to prepare for the upcoming seminar in Florida; he wanted to get to work early and try one more rewrite.

"Don't bother," Polly says. "I'll go." She turns to Charlie. "You."

"I didn't do anything," Charlie quickly says.

"Stay with Amanda," Polly tells him.

"I can't," Charlie groans. "Sevrin's waiting."

"Let him wait," Polly says.

Polly doesn't kiss Ivan good-bye, and she doesn't look at either of them as she grabs her car keys. Charlie and Ivan exchange a guilty look.

"She'll cool off," Ivan says.

Ivan grabs his backpack and follows Polly out, hoping to make up in the driveway. Charlie finishes his French toast, then goes upstairs to look for the net he and Sevrin will need. Amanda's door is open and the room is dark. All the shades have been pulled down. Charlie stops at the door and looks in.

"Hi," Amanda says from under the quilts.

Charlie comes into the room and switches on the light on the night table. "Mom is so crazy about keeping things dark whenever anyone's sick."

"Yeah," Amanda says.

"I'm going to look for my net," Charlie says. "Me and Sevrin are going collecting."

"Good luck," Amanda says.

She's whispering because her sore throat is really bad, the worst she can remember. She feels cold no matter how many quilts are piled on top of her. This is worse than when she had the chicken pox and couldn't sit down, not even to go to the toilet. Worse than when she cried all night because her skin itched.

"Well, go ahead," Amanda tells Charlie. "Go meet Sevrin."

Her throat hurts so much she may start to cry, and she doesn't want Charlie to see.

"I've got to stay with you," Charlie tells her. "Mom," he says apologetically.

"Oh," Amanda says, understanding completely. Her mother's done the same thing with her, forcing her to spend time with Charlie when she doesn't even want to be in the same room with him.

Charlie sits down on a chair near the bed. "Want me to put on a tape for you?" he asks. "Duran Duran?"

Amanda tells him no, she has a headache. They can hear kids down the block, enjoying their freedom.

"Just don't blow your germs this way," Charlie says. "Only ten more days till prison."

That makes Amanda smile. She can't wait for school to start; she's been looking forward to sixth grade all summer. With Helen

Cross graduated and Evelyn Crowley getting sloppy, Amanda will be the best gymnast on the team.

Charlie sits next to her, thinking about horseshoe crabs. If he bikes the long way, and rides along the marsh, he may find some on his way to meet Sevrin. Horseshoe crabs are endlessly fascinating to him, since they were here before the dinosaurs. He cannot understand why no one has discovered the secret of how they managed to survive. Charlie is already half an hour late and Sevrin is probably mad at him by now. His mother does things like this to him all the time, and to Amanda, too. She doesn't understand when they have appointments to keep or phone calls to make. She forgets they have lives of their own.

"I could bring you back a newt," he tells Amanda. "You could keep it in a terrarium."

He realizes then that his sister has fallen asleep. She's holding onto the quilt his mother always covers them with when they're sick. It is blue and white with a border of stars and a few boxes of red in the center. They used to believe it was this quilt that made them well, and if both of them were sick they fought over it. Charlie reaches up and turns off the lamp on the night table. He sits in the chair, his hands on his knees. He finds himself counting the minutes until his mother comes back. In the dark he can see the white stars in the border of the quilt, whiter even than bones.

When twenty-four hours have passed, and Amanda's fever has not gone down, Polly takes her in to be examined. Ed Reardon has been the kids' doctor for seven years, ever since they moved to Morrow. He does a routine throat culture, takes Amanda's temperature, examines her ears, and then, concerned mostly with the swollen lymph nodes he's found all over her body and the girl's weight loss, decides to run some blood and stool tests. He tells Polly they'll have the results back from the lab by tomorrow or the next day, and in the meantime Amanda should continue taking Tylenol. Absolute bed rest, even though Amanda puts up a fight and insists she's feeling better. He would never mention that the first thing he thinks of when he sees symptoms like Amanda's is cancer.

Ed Reardon has seen nearly a dozen kids in the past week with a virus that combines a high fever and vomiting, and he thinks, once again, that he needs a partner and at least one more person on his office staff. He has tomorrow off, and he needs it. He knows he should have longer office hours and spend less time with each patient, his accountant has told him this. But finding a way to see more bodies per hour is not why Ed chose pediatrics. He has three kids himself, a two-year-old son and two daughters, five and eight.

"It's not fair," Amanda says as she gets dressed.

"She's worried about practicing," Polly explains, as she quickly signs the permission slips for all the lab tests. "Gymnastics."

"Don't worry," Ed Reardon tells Amanda. "I can tell just by looking at you. You're better than Mary Lou Retton."

Amanda ducks her head, suddenly shy, but Polly can tell she's pleased. "Thanks," she says to Ed after Amanda has gone to the bathroom to leave urine and stool samples. "She seems better already."

Polly does not add that Ed has made her feel better too. He always does. High fevers make her crazy with fear. Ivan thinks she overreacts, but Ed Reardon listens to her; he seems to trust her instincts.

"She's a great kid," Ed tells Polly.

"I'll bet you say that to all the mothers," Polly teases him.

"I most certainly do not," Ed tells her. "Ten to one her fever subsides by morning."

He's right. Amanda's fever breaks sometime in the night, and by breakfast time her temperature is normal. She's still too tired to do much more than sit on the couch and watch TV, and that suits Charlie since she might have wanted to come to the pond with him and she always wants to go swimming. Amanda doesn't have the patience to watch for specimens.

Charlie and Sevrin filled all the Mason jars with newts yesterday, and last night they sneaked into Sevrin's basement. Half the newts were given sugar-water; the control group had only lettuce and water. But now the boys meet again, back to look for something that got away yesterday. At least Charlie is. Sevrin was busy eating a sandwich and he missed it. He doesn't quite believe that the turtle was at least three feet across.

"Bullshit," Sevrin says now. He is belly down, his hands in the cool water, his knees and bare feet dark with dust. He's brought his dog, a golden retriever named Felix, whom they have to keep on a leash so he won't make a dash for the water. "No turtle could get to be that size in a pond this small."

"A mutant," Charlie suggests. "Maybe someone's been dumping radioactive waste in here."

"Oh, yeah, sure," Sevrin says, echoing his mother's cynical tone. "The one that got away."

"We'll see him," Charlie says. "We'll sit here all day if we have to."

Charlie reaches into his backpack and pulls out two cans of orange soda and two Almond Joys. Sevrin leans back and takes one of the sodas. He snaps the top open loudly.

"Quiet!" Charlie whispers, annoyed.

Sevrin wrinkles his nose and guzzles his orange soda.

It's hot and Charlie takes off his Red Sox T-shirt. If they weren't waiting for the turtle, he'd dive right into the pond. Instead, he holds the cold can of soda against his bare skin.

Blue dragonflies skim over the surface of the water. There's a new housing development through the trees, but the boys aren't aware of it. Small deer still come to the ponds and marshes in Morrow; Charlie knows you can see them at dusk if you're quiet enough.

"Just think, tyrannosauruses might have hung out here," Sevrin muses. "They could have attacked a brontosaurus right here where we're sitting."

Charlie opens his can of soda and drinks deeply. He doesn't bother to tell Sevrin that tyrannosaurus and brontosaurus lived eighty million years apart, and that no fossils of either have been found anywhere near Morrow. Charlie's been told he's a know-it-all enough times for him to have learned when to keep his mouth shut.

Sevrin sits up and takes a candy bar. He puts his feet in the water, and small startled frogs jump into the pond. Sevrin looks back at Charlie apologetically.

"You think our mothers are going to get rich from this book they're doing?" Sevrin asks. Felix sits facing him, panting, waiting for some chocolate to fall. Sevrin finishes his candy bar and puts the crumpled wrapper in his pocket. "Maybe it will be a best-seller. Maybe we'll all be millionaires. Boy, my father will go nuts. He always tells my mom she should go out and get a real job."

"My mom didn't say anything about being a millionaire," Charlie says.

"You know what I'd buy?" Sevrin says. "First a motorcycle, and then a yacht."

Charlie likes being with Sevrin because he doesn't have to talk. Even when Sevrin asks a question, he doesn't necessarily expect an answer. It's been this way since they were three years old. Sevrin dragged his cot next to Charlie's at nursery school and that was it, they were best friends. As far as Charlie is concerned, he never needs another friend as long as he has Sevrin.

"Gonna eat that Almond Joy?" Sevrin asks.

Charlie has taken one bite, but he hands the rest of the candy bar to Sevrin. It's too hot for chocolate; it melts in your hands.

"If I could live on a yacht," Sevrin goes on, between bites of Charlie's candy bar, "I'd never go to school. I'd dive for starfish. I'd never hang up my clothes in the closet because there wouldn't be any closets." He holds out his hands so Felix can lick off the chocolate.

"There wouldn't be any food except Spaghetti-Os," Charlie says.

"Right. Orange soda and Yoo-Hoo to drink."

A kingfisher flies over the pond, and Charlie nudges Sevrin with his foot. Sevrin nods and puts down the sighting in the log he's been keeping for them.

"There'd be a pool on the yacht," Sevrin whispers.

"With one of those curlicue slides," Charlie whispers back.

There is a plunk in the water, as if the kingfisher had dropped a stone into the pond. When Charlie narrows his eyes he sees that the stone is moving. He nudges Sevrin again, and Sevrin automatically looks up, toward the kingfisher.

"I've already got him," Sevrin says.

From this distance it looks like a plank of mossy wood, or an empty barrel. Except that Charlie can see its eyes now. Charlie has not dared to tell Sevrin what he hopes. It's so irrational, so unscientific, but he hopes they have stumbled upon a cryptodire, a turtle that developed in the Triassic period, alongside the dinosaurs, two hundred thirty million years ago. And when he thinks about it, it doesn't really seem so impossible for one to exist when all modern-day turtles are relatives, virtually unchanged from the ones that survived what the dinosaurs could not.

Water sloshes against the thing that looks like a barrel. Charlie kicks Sevrin, hard, and Sevrin turns to him.

"Hey!" Sevrin says.

Charlie nods toward the pond and Sevrin follows his gaze. The turtle is getting closer.

"Holy shit," Sevrin says.

"That's him," Charlie whispers.

Sevrin begins writing furiously in his log. Charlie watches as the turtle gets even closer, before it veers away and dives.

"No one would believe us," Sevrin whispers.

"Who cares," Charlie whispers. "We know what we saw."

They stay for another two hours, forsaking lunch, but the turtle doesn't resurface, or, if it does, it's hidden by weeds. Late in the day they get on their bikes reluctantly and head over to Sevrin's. Unlike many of the houses in Morrow, which are mostly painted white with black or green shutters, Sevrin's house is blue, with yellow trim. There are hanging plants attached to hooks all along the porch, pots of fuchsias and trailing pink geraniums. They leave the dog outside and go into the kitchen. Sevrin and Charlie can hear the furious beat of Betsy's typewriter. The boys move quickly, grabbing a jar of peanut butter, a loaf of bread, four Devil Dogs, and a sack of sugar, and they're down the basement stairs before Betsy can hear them. Betsy often wants to talk to them about something meaningful, when all they want is to be left alone to feed Sevrin's white rat or watch *Star Trek*.

Down in the basement, Sevrin makes the sandwiches while Charlie mixes up more sugar-water for the newts. The turtle is such a spectacular find, they still can't talk about it. Not yet. That's the thing none of their parents understands. You don't have to talk all the time. You can sit right next to each other on old wooden stools and wolf down two peanut butter sandwiches and two Devil Dogs apiece and not have to say a single word.

45

The newts that are being fed sugar-water are looking good, much more energetic than the control group. Charlie makes notes in their log, while Sevrin slaps some peanut butter on the cover of the peanut-butter jar and feeds Cyrus, the rat.

They don't go upstairs until Sevrin's father is home and Betsy calls them up for dinner. Actually, she calls Sevrin, but when she sees Charlie she sets another plate.

"Does your mother know you're here?" Betsy asks Charlie while Sevrin recaps the peanut butter and puts it back in the cabinet.

"Yeah," Charlie says. "She must."

Betsy points to the phone and Charlie calls home. He hates talking on the phone; he doesn't understand what Amanda and Jessie Eagan can possibly find to say for all those hours they talk to each other.

"Tell her you're sleeping over," Sevrin coaches Charlie.

"Ask her," Betsy says pointedly.

Charlie compromises and says, "It's okay if I sleep over," to Polly. It's not really a question, and Charlie knows his mother won't give him any trouble; whenever Charlie or Amanda is sick Polly's so distracted she gives in easily to the one who is well.

"Roger," Charlie says when he hangs up the phone.

"Over and out," Sevrin says as they sit down at the table, waiting to be fed.

"How about you guys helping out," Sevrin's father, Frank, says when he comes into the kitchen.

Sevrin's father is big on asking them to help out, although Charlie has noticed that Frank never seems to do much of that himself.

"We've had an exhausting day," Sevrin tells his father.

"Oh, really?" Frank says.

"Oh, yeah," Sevrin tells him. "A mammoth day."

"A cryptodire of a day," Charlie says, and he and Sevrin both laugh hysterically.

Betsy dishes out reheated lasagna, and when Frank looks displeased she says, "Sorry. I've been working."

Betsy and Frank are going to fight tonight, the boys can tell. They fight over just about anything, Charlie thinks it's sort of like watching TV for them. But that's all right, it will be easier for Sevrin to talk them into letting him and Charlie sleep out in the tent set up in the backyard if they want some privacy. By nine, Frank and Betsy are upstairs in their bedroom, shouting, and Sevrin and Charlie have already set themselves up in the tent with a sleeping bag, two blankets, the five remaining Devil Dogs, a flashlight, and a canteen of cranberry juice.

They've been doing this all summer, sometimes twice a week, with Charlie pointing out all the constellations Ivan has taught him: Orion with his white belt, Aquarius with his luminous pitcher of water. But tonight the sky is so beautiful, so starry and so black, that the boys silently edge closer to one another. It's almost as if they've forgotten all they know, that stars are made of gases and are bigger than the earth. They are beneath a huge, black bowl, transfixed by a million points of light. They're only kids, maybe they shouldn't be out here all alone. Maybe a meteor will plummet to earth and crush their tent, maybe Sirius will fall out of the sky. When they crawl into the tent they agree to keep the flashlight on all night, they let the dog come into the tent with them, despite his snoring, and they sleep close together, their backs pressed up against each other.

It's hot, even at midnight, and Charlie and Sevrin both sleep fitfully, but when they wake up neither admits to ever having been scared. They go into the house and, ignoring the breakfast Betsy left out for them before she went up to her study, eat two uncooked Pop-Tarts apiece.

"Let's not mention the turtle to anyone until we can document the sighting," Charlie says.

"Absolutely," Sevrin agrees.

Charlie knows the best way to prove that the turtle exists is a photograph, but he doesn't know how to get hold of a camera. His mother would never let him touch her Minolta; she treats that camera as if it were gold, and he hasn't seen the old Polaroid for ages.

Charlie has to be home by noon so he can stay with Amanda— be her servant and bring her Tylenol and juice, while his mother finally takes the Blazer in for new shocks. Sevrin rides Charlie halfway home, and they stop where they always do, on the corner of Ash and Chestnut, exactly halfway between their houses.

"I'd better head home," Sevrin says. "If I clean my room my dad may get me a new soccer ball."

Charlie nods his approval, then rolls his bike over the curb.

"See you tomorrow," Sevrin says. He turns his bike around and starts pedaling. "Hey, idiot," he shouts when Charlie doesn't say good-bye. "Adiós."

"Adiós," Charlie calls back.

Charlie pedals hard the rest of the way home. The wind is hot, but it feels good anyway. As he speeds past the Crowleys' house and the Wagoners', Sevrin is going just as fast in the other direction.

That afternoon the heat doesn't let up, and at Pearson's Animal Farm, where Ed Reardon and his wife, Mary, have taken the kids, thick dust rises up and gets into their hair and their clothes. Mary was the one who collected all the stale bread in the breadbox for the ducks and geese, but when they come to the petting zoo she says to Ed, "You go in with them," and then she heads in the other direction so she can collapse on a bench in the shade.

Ed's daughters beg for quarters so they can feed the baby llama with bottles. His son, Will, clings to his legs, frightened of the pygmy goats that run up and surround them, nuzzling and pushing, searching for bread.

"They can't hurt you," Ed tells his son.

Just to show Will how gentle the goats are, Ed reaches to pat one on the head and gets butted for his troubles. He picks Will up so he can toss bread down for the goats without fear of being trampled. In the shade, Mary undoes several buttons on her blouse and fans herself with her hand. Ed watches her, puzzled, then he realizes what he's seeing. From this distance she looks displeased. Happiness has come easily to them, they haven't had to struggle for it, but lately they've had silences, and these lapses make Ed suspicious of their happiness. He can tell Mary things that upset him terribly—as he did last night, when he mentioned Amanda Farrell's disturbingly low white blood count and his decision to run a series of tests, tests whose positive results would be disastrous—and get no response whatsoever from Mary. Does she not listen to him? Has she heard so many stories about his patients that she simply tunes him out?

"Are you all right?" Ed asks Mary when the children have had enough of the petting zoo and are ready for the small carousel and the bumper cars.

"Of course I am," Mary says. She pulls Will onto her lap and feels in his diaper to see if he needs a change. He was potty-trained for a week and has had a temporary setback.

Ed's beeper goes off and he quickly reaches to turn it off.

"We'll meet you at the carousel," Mary says.

"Sorry," Ed says. He says this every time he's called away by his service.

"If I'm not used to it by now, I never will be," Mary says, but still, Ed wonders. Sometimes he thinks that Mary blames him for his patients' illnesses, that she half believes he uses his work as an excuse to get away from his own family.

Ed plans to make it fast and get back before the kids are off the carousel, but he has to search for a pay phone. Finally he spies one behind the refreshment stand. It's three o'clock, nap

49

time, and children all over Pearson's Animal Farm are cranky, refusing to walk, demanding ice cream, being scolded by their parents. When he phones his service he's told that the lab wants to speak with him directly. He has to search his pockets for change and he's sorry now that he gave his daughters all his quarters. The phone feels too cold in his hand; the buttons stick as he punches in the number for the lab. He knows something is wrong, he can feel it by the way the air crackles with heat. Ed makes them repeat it twice: An organism called cryptosporidium has been found in Amanda's stool sample. That's what's been causing her diarrhea, but Ed know this is just an opportunistic disease. He feels dizzy even before he's told that Amanda Farrell, whom he has seen through chicken pox, ear infections, and inoculations, as well as a broken arm and a worrisome appendectomy, has tested positive for AIDS. Ed Reardon, a graduate of Harvard Medical School, who completed both his internship and residency at Children's Hospital in Boston and who has been in private practice for twelve years, sits down on the ground behind the refreshment stand that serves lemonade and popcorn.

He doesn't plan to move for a long time.

That night is quiet, there is no longer the chorus of katydids that rang through the air all summer. The heat breaks suddenly, at midnight; a thread of thin, milky clouds makes a ring around the moon. It's amazing that nightmares don't travel through a town the way chicken pox does, swept through open windows, slipping around the corners of doors left ajar.

Ivan loves cool weather, so he gets a particularly good night's sleep and the next morning he's at the institute before nine. The institute is in a small house directly across from the town green, a circle of grass bordered by hostas and late-blooming lilies, which was once used as a communal grazing area. Out by the marsh, near Red Slipper Beach, is the domelike building that houses the telescope. Charlie now takes the huge telescope for granted, but Ivan can remember the amazed look on Charlie's face when he first saw the ceiling open to reveal the sky. Usually, Ivan drives down to Red Slipper Beach once a night, although lately the graduate students have been doing most of the viewing as the astronomers prepare their papers. Ivan has a lot of preparing to do before the Orlando conference. His particular interest is the supernova, and one has just occurred. Actually, it occurred one hundred seventy thousand years ago, but it has just now been sighted over South America. Ivan can't help wondering whether, if he were affiliated with MIT or Stanford instead of the poorly funded institute, he might be in Chile right now, instead of getting information secondhand at the conference. Ivan is not used to feeling dissatisfied and it eats at him. There are four astronomers at the institute, five graduate students, and two secretaries. He has always liked the intensity of the place, the smallness. Now he wonders if perhaps he hasn't settled for second best.

When he was young, Ivan seemed like an affable, even-tempered boy, but he wasn't. From the time he was ten he had two plans of action: to become a scientist and to get out of New Jersey and away from his family. He still considers his acceptance to MIT his salvation. Both of his parents are dead, but his two sisters, Ilene and Natalie, still live in Fairlawn. They see each other every weekend, and Nat and her family live in the big brick house where they grew up. Ivan knows they talk about him—he overheard a remark in the kitchen of the old house after his father's funeral. Actually, it was Polly they were blasting, because she wore no makeup and no jewelry other than her wedding ring, but it might as well have been a direct attack upon Ivan. What it comes down to, Ivan knows, is that he and his sisters grew up in the same house but have always inhabited different worlds.

They still cannot understand what Ivan does for a living, or why he does it. How they can be made from the same genetic material and be so completely different is more of a mystery to Ivan than any riddle in this galaxy or any other. And maybe that's why Charlie brings him such pleasure. Not that Ivan loves one of his children more than the other, but Charlie is like him. He cares about clouds and constellations; he may not listen when he's told to clean his room, but he always listens to the sound of crickets in the tall grass, he never fails to keep watch for changes in the sky.

Ivan is at his desk before any of his colleagues, with a hot cup of coffee and a buttered roll he picked up on the way. He is looking at the data from their computer, tied into NASA, when the phone rings. He doesn't bother to answer until one of the secretaries, Monica, buzzes him, and then he knows it's for him. He guesses that it's Polly, calling to remind him of something he's forgotten—he's been doing a lot of forgetting these days—but it's a man's voice, one he doesn't recognize.

"It's Ed," the voice tells him.

"Ed," Ivan repeats, and it takes him a moment before he can place this Ed as the kids' doctor.

"I'd like you to come in this morning," Ed says.

Ivan wonders if they owe Dr. Reardon for the kids' last checkup. He knows he paid the mortgage this month, and the electric company, but more than that he cannot remember.

"How about ten?" Ed says.

"The hell of it is," Ivan says, "I've got a paper to finish before Friday. Have you tried Polly? She's got the checkbook anyway."

All morning, Ed has been telling himself it would be easier to tell Ivan alone, without Polly; a scientist could better accept the random path of a virus. Now he knows he's been kidding himself. No one can accept the indiscriminate order of cruelty. No one can even begin to explain it, and yet this is exactly what he has to try to do.

"How about ten-thirty?" Ed Reardon presses.

"Come on, Ed," Ivan kids him. "Don't you think I'm a little old for your practice?"

There is silence on the other end of the wire. Ivan can hear his own heartbeat.

"All right," Ivan says. "I'm leaving now."

He tells Monica he'll be back after lunch, then stops into Max Lyman's office and tells him he can't play squash this week. It takes him less than fifteen minutes to get over to Reardon's office. He tells the nurse, the blond one, that he's here, and she quickly goes into the doctor's office. Does he imagine that she looks uncomfortable? Does he imagine the edge of panic?

The waiting room is crowded. Ivan finds a space on the couch, but he feels too big for the room. He hasn't been here with either of the kids for over a year, and he can't quite remember whether that's because the kids have been healthy or because Polly's taken over that job. The first few years they'd been here constantly, with both Charlie and Amanda. Ear infections, mainly. For a while it seemed there wasn't a month when one of the kids didn't have one.

Ed Reardon comes out, walks right to him, and shakes his hand firmly.

"Let's go into my office," Ed says. He doesn't let go of Ivan's hand.

A toddler lets out a yelp as soon as he sees the doctor, and her mother holds her so she can't run out of the office.

"I can see you're a popular guy," Ivan jokes.

Ed opens the door to his office and motions for Ivan to go in first. Ivan can feel himself being watched as he sits down in a chair facing the desk. And that's when he knows something is wrong.

Later, as he drives home, Ivan will pull over to the side of the road, not far from where there are wild raspberries Polly and the children like to pick every summer. He has been crying since he left Ed Reardon's office, but now he begins to howl. It is a terrifying sound. It comes from deep inside him, but it doesn't seem to belong to him, he can hear it from the outside, as if it were somebody else's pain. All the mornings when he could not wait to leave the house and get to the institute come back to him, the times when he was too tired to see who was crying in the middle of the night and sent Polly to check, the spilled milk, the annoying sound of cartoons on Saturdays, the vacations he and Polly have planned, just the two of them, so they could get away.

When the howling stops, Ivan sits motionless behind the steering wheel and he holds onto it. It crosses his mind that he should kill Ed Reardon. Ed is the one who diagnosed Amanda's appendicitis. There was unexpected bleeding during her surgery; Ivan remembers being told she needed a transfusion. That was when she was given the contaminated blood. For five years Ivan has been losing her without knowing it. Every time he has sent her to her room for being fresh, every time he missed a gymnastics meet, every hour he has spent looking at dead stars, he has been losing her.

And now, on a Thursday morning, as blackbirds light on the brambles that grow alongside the road, he has lost her.

4

THEY CAN HEAR traffic out on the street. Amanda is wearing white jeans and a T-shirt patterned with clouds; her hair is pulled back with two barrettes shaped like Scotties. On this doctor's desk there is a container of jelly beans, the expensive kind with flavors like blueberry and chocolate and mint. The doctor is pretty and Amanda likes the earrings she wears, slices of silver moons that swing back and forth each time the doctor moves her head.

"Do you understand what a virus is?" the doctor asks. She is a specialist in pediatric AIDS named Ellen Shapiro.

Amanda nods her head yes. She looks so serious, the way she does in class when she has to learn a lesson on which she'll later be tested. Polly forces herself to look away from her daughter. In a hard-backed chair, on the other side of Amanda, Ivan is motionless; he's like a man made out of stone. The window is open and the city sounds of Boston are jarring to someone used to the quiet of Morrow. In Morrow, the wind makes more noise than anything else; it rattles the leaves from the trees in November, it whooshes down the chimneys on wild January nights and breaks the thin, blue icicles off the rain gutters. A long time ago, ages ago, when Polly was a little girl in New York, she never noticed the sounds of traffic. Now, she hears not only the traffic but also something underneath the whir of engines and the horns honking. She could swear it was the sound of someone screaming.

Polly and Ivan have made a vow not to cry in front of Amanda, and they've kept to it, but when they're alone they break down suddenly, they find themselves weeping when they brush their teeth, when they reach for socks in a dresser drawer. They do not think about why it is that they haven't touched once since Ivan locked the bedroom door and told Polly, or why they both have this horrible feeling of culpability, as if there must have been something they could have done to prevent this, if only they had been better parents.

Yesterday, before they told Amanda, they sent Charlie on the bus down to New York to visit Polly's parents. It was more than just wanting to protect him; the presence of any healthy child, even Charlie, makes what is happening to Amanda realer. They constantly consider the possibility of a misdiagnosis, but when they lie in bed at night, without touching, each feels completely without hope.

When they told her, she stared at them as though they'd gone crazy.

"No, I'm not," Amanda had said, puzzled. "I'm not sick."

While Ivan explained about the blood transfusion and the virus, Amanda chewed bubble gum and stared at the ceiling. When he was done, she sighed and said, "All right. How much school do I have to miss?"

"We don't know about school," Ivan had said.

The look Amanda gave him raised goosebumps along Polly's skin.

"What!" Amanda had shouted. "You have to know."

Polly tried to put her arms around her, but Amanda bolted from the table. She stood between the sink and the refrigerator, cornered, a wild look in her eye.

"I can't be sick!" Amanda screamed at them. "Don't you understand anything! I can't miss school!"

She ran up to her room and locked herself in, and they let her. They let her sit in the dark and cry, they let her listen to one cassette tape after another, and when she came back downstairs at a little after nine that night, they nodded when she said her eyes might look funny because she was tired. They sat around the kitchen table, eating chocolate ice cream. But they didn't look at each other; they didn't dare speak above a whisper. They've become sleepwalkers, wandering through their own nightmares, each avoiding the others for fear that a word, a conversation, a kiss will make them realize they aren't dreaming.

This morning, before they set off for Boston, Polly made a pot of strong coffee. She poured herself a cup, but she couldn't drink it. The house was much too quiet; it was like the house in a dream that even the dreamer knows is not quite right simply because the edges of things blur. Polly is afraid that if she reaches for a coffee cup her hand will go through a wall, if she turns on the tap instead of water out will come spiders and stones. This is the kind of dream where everything too terrible to imagine suddenly happens, it happens when your back is turned, just when you think everything is fine.

When the phone rang, Polly answered before she thought better of it. It was Betsy Stafford, calling to give her hell.

"If you're playing at being a photographer, just tell me," Betsy had said, without giving Polly a chance to say anything. "I'll get someone else to work with me."

Polly was so numb she hadn't recognized Betsy's voice and

she had recoiled from the phone in shock, wondering if someone was making an obscene phone call.

"We had a meeting yesterday and you weren't there. No phone call. No appearance. No nothing."

Polly realized then who it was, but she still could not speak. When she opened her mouth her tongue felt cottony. At the time when Polly should have been at Laurel Smith's cottage she and Ivan were meeting with Ed Reardon to discuss the series of diagnostic tests scheduled at Children's Hospital. Twice, Polly had to hold Ivan back, or he would have attacked Ed. And even then, when Ivan promised to hear Ed out, he was shaking, ready to erupt. He had a crazy look on his face, like a madman behind the wheel who's just waiting for someone to cut him off on the road so he can pull his gun. It was terrifying to see Ivan look this way; he is the least violent person Polly has ever known, he won't kill an ant, he'll calmly back down from most arguments. It's not a question of Ivan's not knowing his own size and strength, he's simply not built to fight. He'd worry too much about the other guy. But there, in the doctor's office, Ivan kept cracking his knuckles; he wasn't looking anyone in the eye. He has already told Polly that, as far as he's concerned, Amanda's been murdered. He is looking for suspects; if he could ever find out who donated the blood Amanda got, he would break that person's neck, he would listen to the bones snap. He'll never find that person, but from the way he was acting, it appeared that Ed Reardon was the next best thing. He seemed not to be listening as Ed and Polly discussed how important it was to Amanda that she stay in school, but he was still making that awful sound with his knuckles, and then, for no reason at all, he stood up suddenly and, facing Ed, shouted, "God damn you!"

Polly finds herself thinking about that crazy look on Ivan's face more often than she should. She was thinking about it all the while Betsy was yelling at her; she couldn't stop herself, it was like something stuck in her brain and she had to replay that one image of Ivan, again and again.

"This morning you were supposed to be at my place at eight-thirty to go over the latest proofs," Betsy told her. "What the hell have you been doing? Making breakfast for your kids?"

"Amanda's sick," Polly had said then.

"Well, then call me!" Betsy said. "Let me know when we can reschedule. Show some shred of professionalism. Meanwhile, Laurel had an amazing reading. This new client of hers is so uptight that she was floored by the experience and I had to lend her a Valium."

"She's really sick," Polly said.

"What do you mean?" Betsy said.

"She has AIDS," Polly said. It was the first time she had said the word aloud. It seemed an impossible word, one she shouldn't even know.

"She had a transfusion five years ago. They say she has AIDS."

There was complete silence on the other end of the phone. Finally Betsy said, "Oh, my God. It's not possible."

"No," Polly had said. "It's not possible."

"Forget about the book," Betsy had told her. "Forget about it until this whole thing is over."

Polly did not like the sound of that. When she looked down at her own hands they looked old. She could have been looking at her mother's hands.

"All right," Polly agreed.

"Oh, Christ," Betsy said then. "I forgot that Charlie was supposed to come over today. I have to take Sevrin for new shoes. School," she explained. "He has to have Reeboks."

"Charlie's in New York. We sent him to my parents'. We can't tell him yet."

59

"Of course not," Betsy had said. "Especially when it may all blow over. That happens all the time. My mother was diagnosed as having breast cancer. They wanted to operate immediately, but my mother, in her usual difficult manner, said absolutely not. They gave her a year at most to live, and that was eight years ago. Shows you how much doctors know."

But this doctor at Children's Hospital seems to know quite a lot. She explains the AIDS virus to Amanda matter-of-factly.

"An immune system is what keeps you healthy," Ellen Shapiro says. "It's like an army that helps fight off viruses."

"I don't understand," Amanda says.

"Well, without that army, that immune system, the body is more likely to pick up diseases. It can't fight off infections. AIDS shuts down the immune system and leaves you open to diseases you wouldn't get if you hadn't been infected with AIDS."

"I understand that," Amanda says. She leans forward in her chair. "I don't understand why kids get it."

Polly can't stop herself before something escapes from inside her. She coughs to disguise the sob. Ivan looks over at her; he has that same strange look so that his eyes are blank. He told Polly once about seeing a dog run over on Route 16; when he got out of his car and saw the blood he felt as though he himself were drained, as though there were nothing inside him.

Ellen Shapiro gets up and comes around to their side of the desk. She sits on the edge of the desk and puts her hand on Amanda's shoulder.

"I don't either," she says.

Amanda jerks away from Ellen Shapiro, her face flushed with anger. "You should," Amanda says. "Doctors are supposed to know."

"It's a new disease," Ellen Shapiro says gently. "We're learning more about it all the time."

"I don't want to talk about this anymore," Amanda says. She turns to her mother. "I don't want to be here anymore."

"All right," Polly says.

And why should Amanda have to stay here? A team headed by Dr. Shapiro has already examined her. They have found two small lesions in her mouth, at the base of her tongue, and they've agreed with Ed Reardon's observation that her glands and lymph nodes are swollen, her muscles inflamed. No one had to tell Polly that Amanda has lost close to ten pounds; she can tell that by the way Amanda's clothes hang loosely. The white jeans Amanda wears used to be so tight Polly had to help her with the zipper. Now the jeans are cinched with a woven blue belt.

"I'll be working with your doctor at home," Ellen Shapiro says.

"That's comforting," Ivan says. "That makes my day."

Ellen Shapiro writes down her phone number on a yellow pad, tears off the paper, and hands it to Polly. "You can call me anytime you have questions. I hope you will."

"You think you can answer our questions?" Ivan says.

"You have to understand that this is nobody's fault," Ellen Shapiro says. When Ivan looks away, the doctor turns to Polly. "You know that."

"I know it," Polly says.

She doesn't blame Ed Reardon for diagnosing Amanda's appendicitis. In fact, she feels comforted by Ed; she's taken to calling him several times a day.

Why is it that she still feels that someone, something, must be to blame?

Out in the hallway, Polly puts one arm over Amanda's shoulders as they walk toward the elevator. They follow behind Ivan, and Polly thinks about how annoying it was when she and Ivan would go out on a date and he'd walk so quickly she'd have to struggle to keep up with him. She used to tease him and say he got into the habit of walking so fast because as a boy he wanted to get away from his family so badly; he was looking for giant steps to get him out of New Jersey. Over the years, Ivan has slowed his pace, but sometimes when he's with the children Polly has noticed that they have to run or be left behind.

"Let's just get out of here," Ivan says when they reach the elevator. "Let's go out for pizza."

Polly stares at him.

"I'm serious," Ivan says. "We'll go to the North End."

Amanda looks at the floor and starts to cry.

"Honey," Polly says, but Amanda turns away from her. "Great idea," Polly says to Ivan. "Just fabulous."

Ivan ignores Polly. He goes over to Amanda and leans down so he can whisper. "What do you say we just go home?" he says.

"Yeah," Amanda says, her voice thick.

Polly hits the down button for the elevator. They won't be able to keep Charlie out of this any longer; it's going to take over their lives. Polly knows she's a coward, but she's going to ask her father to tell Charlie. She just can't do it, and she's afraid to ask Ivan, afraid of what he'll say to a little boy.

"I shouldn't have been so mean to that doctor," Amanda says. Her voice is small, the way it always is after she's cried.

"She didn't seem to mind," Polly says.

Polly thinks she may dissolve if the elevator doesn't come soon. They keep this hospital much too hot; there is always the sound of metal, wheels creaking, machinery, bedpans and food trays hitting against each other on shiny silver carts. She will do whatever she can to keep Amanda out of here.

"I just shouldn't have talked to her that way," Amanda says. "I have to be nice to her."

They are standing in front of the elevator. Polly turns Amanda so that they're facing each other.

"You don't have to be nice to anyone you don't want to be nice to," Polly tells her.

"I'd better," Amanda says. "If I want her to cure me."

Amanda steps into the elevator when the doors open, and Polly and Ivan follow her in. Ivan pushes the button for the lobby, and as the elevator begins its descent, Polly allows herself one dizzying moment of hope. She leans toward Ivan; she's missed him. Falling together through space, they reach for each other and hold hands, and they don't let go until they get to the lobby.

That night Amanda realizes she is afraid of the dark. She switches on the light in her closet and leaves the door open. She turns on her desk lamp and then gets into bed, but she can't close her eyes. Things look strange. The belts on a hook in her closet look more like black snakes, her old stuffed animals up on the shelf above her dresser look scary, they look as if their eyes are moving around in their heads.

Amanda forces herself to stay in bed and keep her head on her pillow. She tries an old trick her mother once taught her, when she was little and prone to nightmares. She will only think about things she likes; she will make a list of a hundred wonderful things, and, if she's lucky, she will be asleep before she runs out of wonderful things.

Soon it will be impossible to sleep with the windows open, except for those few miraculous Indian summer nights when the moon is orange and the air is deceitful and warm. But now, it's still summer, at least on the calendar. It's good to think about apple pies, and silver gypsy bracelets, and pink silk bathrobes, the kind with lace that are too expensive to buy. It's good to think about rabbits on the grass and the way her father smiles when they meet someone on the street and he introduces her as his daughter. Someday she'll drink beer, she'll have a scarlet dress with a wide silver belt, and earrings so long they'll brush her shoulders.

Late that night, sometime after midnight, after Amanda has fallen asleep, and Ivan has turned one last time and finally fallen asleep as well, Polly gets out of bed and pulls on a pair of jeans and an old gray T-shirt. She's very quiet when she walks down the hall; she doesn't make a sound. The only problem is that she doesn't know where she's going. The dishes have all been rinsed off and put in the dishwasher. There's no point in pretending to have a cup of tea. Standing in the kitchen, in the dark, Polly hears the squeak of an exercise wheel from the basement and remembers that Charlie asked her to feed his specimens. She switches on the dim stairway light and goes downstairs. It smells like animals and earth; Polly wonders what the mice that run through their house think when they come upon this section of the basement and find Charlie's hamsters and field mice in their warm cages, so lazy and well nourished.

The field mice stare at Polly as she gets out their bag of food. They're not white, like pet store mice, but small and brown with black eyes; if one ran across the floor you'd think it was a shadow, nothing more.

Tonight, Charlie is sleeping at her parents' house in Polly's old room, which was turned into a den years ago, with a pull-out couch for overnight visitors. Polly used to have an oak spindle bed that her father, Al, found at a flea market out on Long Island. Polly watched him refinish the bed on weekends, down in the basement of the building where he was, and still is, the superintendent. It was warm down there in all seasons, because of the hot-water pipes that ran overhead. Al usually gave two or three half-wild cats free run of the basement, to chase away "mouse cousins," and his cats, which were often large and mean, certainly seemed ready, willing, and able should a rat ever be stupid enough to cross them. Al swiped things from the kitchen for them, cans of tunafish, Swiss cheese, chicken wings. He called the cats his "boys," regardless of their sex, and he always said to Polly, "Let's not mention the boys' dinner to your mother," when they took a stolen treat down to the basement.

Polly still wonders if she should have realized that something was wrong between her parents, but what happened to them seemed as much a surprise to Al as to anyone else. On weekends in the summer he went out to Long Island, to Blue Point, to go fishing, and one Sunday he didn't come back. Polly remembers what she and her mother had for dinner that night: meatloaf, roasted potatoes, and lima beans. There was Jell-O for dessert, the kind only Al liked, with chunks of pineapple in it.

"We'll just save your father's dinner," Polly's mother, Claire, had said.

Claire wrapped the plate in aluminum foil and put it in the refrigerator, where it stayed for four days before she finally threw it out. When tenants called up, Claire lied and said Al was sick with the flu and wouldn't be able to fix the pipes or paint the hallway until the following week. She wrote down every complaint on a piece of yellow paper, which she kept by the phone.

"What if he doesn't come back?" Polly asked her mother.

"We'll just tell them he's still down with the flu," Claire told her.

When Polly was in bed she could hear her mother crying, but in the mornings Claire never said a word against Al, never acted as if the morning were anything unusual now that it was just the two of them at the table eating eggs. One night, Polly woke up suddenly, in a sweat. She got out of bed, she had a lump in her throat, and when she went into the living room all the lights were on, but the apartment was empty. There was no one in her parents' bedroom, in the kitchen, or the bathroom. She was alone, they had both left her.

Polly knew she couldn't stay in that empty apartment. She could feel her heart pounding. She put her shoes on and pulled a sweater over her nightgown; she took five dollars from a secret place she knew about under the sink. She was breathing hard and she may have been crying, but she wasn't about to wait around for them, not when they'd left her. She could starve all alone, she could die of thirst.

Their apartment was on the first floor, so once she was out in the hallway, all Polly had to do was walk through the heavy double doors onto the street, walk two blocks east, and she'd be at the police station. She would turn herself in as an orphan, and they'd know what to do with her. But out in the hallway she saw that the metal door to the basement was ajar and that the lights were on. Polly slipped through the door and listened for robbers, but all she heard was a tapping sound. She didn't think about cockroaches or rats. She followed the sound down the stairs.

Claire was kneeling down, spooning cat food onto the old chipped plates Al kept down there. The cats were crouched in a corner, watching suspiciously. When she realized someone was watching her, Claire looked up and blinked. "The boys," she explained.

"You should have let them starve," Polly told her mother.

"Polly!" Claire said.

"That's what you should have done," Polly said.

By the time Al came back, nine days later, Polly hated him. He was visiting a friend, he said, but Polly knew it was a lady friend. She had a little house in Blue Point, with a lawn and a hedge of evergreens. Al had actually taken Polly there once, and she'd waited in the car for nearly an hour, finally falling asleep with her cheek pressed up against the scratchy upholstery.

"Great fishing in Blue Point," Al said when he came back.

"I'm sure," Claire said.

"I couldn't stay there," Al said.

"So I see," Claire said and, because it was nearly dinner, she took out some carrots and potatoes to peel.

"That's it?" Polly had said to her mother. "You're taking him back?"

"Don't think you understand everything about grownups, because you don't," Al told Polly.

Polly ignored her father. She watched as her mother searched through a drawer for her vegetable peeler. She hated her father, but what she felt for Claire was worse. She didn't know what it was called, but it was pity, and it changed something between them forever. Even now, Polly cannot look at her mother without thinking of the night her father came home, and so she stays away. She sees her parents as little as possible, and she prefers to go visit them instead of having them come up. That way, she can always leave. But tonight, as she sits in her own basement, she thinks more kindly of her father than she has in years. She thinks of what he taught her: how to change a washer, how to check the underside of a painted dresser drawer and know if it's made out of oak or pine, how not to be afraid of dark basements, of the noise steam pipes make when they moan and send up heat. Tonight Charlie is asleep in her old room, where the pattern of headlights on the wall used to be as comforting to Polly as fireflies are now, and Polly hopes that tonight, at least, her son sleeps well.

In the morning, no one has to wake Charlie or call him for breakfast. He's dressed and ready by eight, and he's one of the first inside the Museum of Natural History. It's nice and cold in the museum, and Charlie's breath fogs up the glass as he peers into cases of fossils. He loves coming to the museum; it's the best part about visiting his grandparents, who live just two blocks away. Usually, his grandfather lets him wander around by himself. Today his grandfather accompanies him from room to room, but that's all right. It's not as if he were with his mother, who would talk the whole time.

Charlie's grandfather appreciates the museum, the smell of it, the darkness, the way footsteps echo. Charlie has begged his parents to let him come to New York on the bus, and they've always said no, but now his mother was the one to suggest he go alone. He plans to get Sevrin something from the gift shop, as an apology for not phoning to let him know he wouldn't be around to take care of the newts. Sevrin has never been to New York and has only been to the Peabody Museum in Cambridge. Charlie plans to get him a patch his mom can sew on his jacket, something tremendously cool—he's seen some that glow in the dark.

"Look at those bones," Charlie's Grandpa Al says every once in a while, as they move from the brontosaurus to the allosaurus. Finally, in front of the tyrannosaurus, he adds, "What a monster."

When they have been in the museum for a little more than two hours, Charlie's grandfather says, "My feet hurt. Let's take a break."

They haven't gotten to many of Charlie's favorite exhibits, haven't even taken a peek at the mammals, but Charlie's grandfather can't be talked into staying. The one thing Charlie insists on is stopping at the gift shop. There he buys a tyrannosaurus patch for Sevrin and then, on impulse, another just like it for himself. It's not exactly to show they have a private club; they're too old for that sort of thing. It's just a badge of their devotion to science. Charlie pays the cashier, then finds his grandfather, who's waiting for him at the door.

"Can we come back later?" Charlie asks.

It's hot outside and, after the darkness of the museum, Charlie and Al both blink in the sunlight. The smell of soot and gas fumes hits them.

"Maybe," Al says. He's never been a good liar. "Probably not."

"Okay," Charlie says. "What about tomorrow? We could spend the whole day here tomorrow."

"Let's sit," Al says.

They head for some benches and Grandpa Al sits. Charlie intends to sit, but it's impossible to resist the ledge behind the bench. Just as he's about to climb up, Al pats the bench with the cupped palm of his hand.

"Right next to me," Charlie's grandfather tells him.

Charlie sits right next to him, and Al puts his arm around him and squeezes his shoulder.

"I got a call from your mother," Al says. "I'm going to drive you home tomorrow."

Charlie looks at him, feeling betrayed. He just got in last night, and this is what he gets? Two hours at the museum?

"This isn't fair," Charlie says.

"No," Al says, "it isn't."

This is exactly why it's impossible to have a fight with Grandpa Al; he always agrees with you.

"Amanda is sick," Al says. "That's why I'm taking you home."

Charlie is wearing old high-topped sneakers. He suddenly realizes that his sneakers are too small. He can feel them cutting into the flesh above his ankle bones.

"How sick?" Charlie says.

"It's very bad," Al tells him. "It's a virus called AIDS."

Charlie stands up and faces the museum. "I know what AIDS is, I know it's a virus."

"She got it from a blood transfusion," Al says. "Before they knew about AIDS, before they tested for contaminated blood."

Charlie bites his lip until he draws blood. He is an idiot. He should have known something was wrong when his mother let him come to New York alone. Al comes up behind Charlie and stands close by. Charlie can feel the subway beneath them, he can feel the heat from the sewers. He cannot help wondering if there's been some mistake.

Maybe it should have happened to him.

That night, Charlie has trouble falling asleep, and when he does he dreams he is no longer human. He dreams there are red stars overhead and bursts of fire. The earth shakes with something deep within itself. He thinks *water,* because he can smell it. Water means warm, so he tracks the smell. He is lucky to be alive; the eggs of the others like him were more exposed to the cold, and each one froze.

He has trouble remembering anything before now. What it was like following the thing that was like him but bigger, feeding on whatever it left behind, panicking whenever he lost the scent of the thing that was like him but bigger because he knew, if he lost it, it would never turn around to look for him. Turning around, stopping, means the end.

At the very beginning, there were the eggs of the others for him to eat until he could follow the thing that was like him but bigger. They were together until the thing that was like him but bigger wouldn't let him near its kill and he struck out at it. He heard a roar from his own throat, and he was so hungry that he wouldn't give up. The thing that was like him but bigger ran away, leaving behind a pool of blood. He was alone then, he no longer followed the thing that was like him because it was no longer bigger.

He knows enough to keep going. Sometimes, he is almost
tricked by sunlight. He lies down and feels it soak into his body,
feels it could nourish him, but if he stays in one place too long
the cold will kill him. There are times when he kills his food,
but more often he eats what he finds. Things that no longer
move because they have been frozen. He breaks his nails tearing
apart their frozen hides. He searches inside their bodies for some
warm core, perhaps a den of flesh to sleep in, but he finds nothing
that brings him comfort.

Everywhere he goes there were once swamps, water so warm
steam rose from the reeds. Things were alive. There was heat,
things smaller to kill and eat, endless green plants. That was
before his time. He has always been cold. He feels black inside;
outside, scales fall from him and freeze as they hit the ground.
He doesn't look up anymore when he hears things explode in
the sky. He used to run and hide. He used to claw at the hard,
cold earth. Now he just keeps moving. Now he is going toward
water. He is looking for something warm. He cannot eat enough
to fill his huge body. When he sees others like him he is ready
to fight if he has to, but he doesn't want to use up his strength,
so he waits and often the others look at him and flee.

Tyrant lizard is what he will be called, *Tyrannosaurus rex*. But
he is no tyrant; he has trouble lifting his legs to walk because
the cold starts at the bottom and goes all the way up. Water.
He can smell it. He keeps following the scent, the same way he
used to follow the thing that was like him but bigger. The
earth he walks on is as cold as ever; a thin layer of ice clings to
his back and tail, but somewhere, deep inside him, there is still
heat.

Charlie wakes near dawn, terrified by the sound of his own
heart pounding. He puts his hands on his chest; his skin feels
hot through his pajamas. He counts backward from one hundred

and, as he does, his heart stops racing. He falls back into a dreamless sleep, and later, when he wakes up, he's still tired. He can't stop thinking about his dream. He dawdles over breakfast, he watches TV till noon, he takes his time at lunch and forces himself to have two grilled cheese sandwiches not because he's hungry, but to waste time.

Late in the afternoon, Charlie's grandmother sews one of the tyrannosaurus patches on his denim jacket, while his grandfather gets the cooler and packs apples and cheese and beer for the ride. The apartment has old air conditioners, which hum loudly. The slipcovers on the couches are bordered with large pink roses. Charlie's grandmother will not be driving up with them. She has pointedly not been invited. Claire knows Polly is afraid she'll break down; Polly has never forgiven her disappointments that happened so long ago Claire doesn't even remember what they were.

Charlie notices that his grandmother's hands shake as she sews on the patch. She was once a seamstress at Bendel's, but her stitches are not as small as they used to be. Charlie kisses her good-bye when she finishes the jacket.

"Don't you dare turn around and drive back tonight," Claire tells her husband.

"Do you think I'm crazy?" Al says, and he winks at Charlie.

Charlie's grandfather has been the building super for thirty-five years. He has his own parking space in the small underground garage, he knows nearly everyone on the block, at least the old-timers, and he can fix almost anything or, at least, make it seem that he has until the next time it breaks down. He built Charlie his first hamster cage, out of wood and chicken wire, and he has several strange habits: he drinks hot water with lemon at breakfast, he refuses to watch a movie made after 1952, and he always drinks a beer when he drives out of Manhattan. The beer is the tangible object that separates the city and Al's never-ending duties as super. It is what, before today, has always seemed like freedom. Once they've gone over the Triborough Bridge, Al asks Charlie to open a bottle of beer.

"It's just as well your grandmother's not coming with us," he tells Charlie. "She doesn't handle illnesses well. Although, as far as she's concerned, doctors can cure anything. I always tell her she should have married a doctor. Mind if I smoke a cigar?"

The smell makes Charlie sick, but he says, "Sure," and gets one from the glove compartment. His grandfather isn't allowed to smoke at home; he has to sit in the basement if he wants a cigar. Al hands Charlie the cold bottle of beer to hold, then takes the cigar and lights it.

"Do you think she'll die?" Charlie says.

"Well, son," his grandfather says, "we're all going to die, aren't we?"

"Don't talk to me like I'm a baby," Charlie says.

"You're right," Al says. "I forget how old you are. As far as I can tell, it doesn't look good." He glances at Charlie to gauge his reaction. "Want to try that beer?"

Charlie looks over at his grandfather to see if he's kidding. Al's eyes are on the road. Charlie takes a swig of beer, which stings as it goes down. It is disgusting. Charlie wipes his mouth with the back of his hand.

"Not bad," he says.

They take the turnoff for the New England Thruway. Charlie stares out the window and imagines the tyrannosaurus in his dream. It is taller than any of the trees along the road, taller than the lampposts and the water towers. The sky is clear, the luminous blue it turns on summer evenings, just before dark.

Charlie thinks of teeth and claws, blood and bones. He always thought he was smart, and now, quite suddenly, he sees that science has made him stupid. He really believed that, given enough time, science could answer any question, but it cannot answer what is most important: What if there's no time left?

"I've been up and down this road so many times, I know it by heart," Grandpa Al says. "Want some music?"

"I don't want to go home," Charlie says.

"Of course you don't," Al says, his foot steady on the gas.

They drive the rest of the way in silence except for the few songs Charlie's grandfather sings, old songs Charlie doesn't know the words to, love songs Al himself can barely remember. After they skirt Boston, the air begins to feel salty. They drive on 95, past Peabody, and Gloucester, and Ipswich. At the exit for Morrow, they see three white herons walking along the side of the road. Charlie's grandfather switches on the high beams and he has a second beer, not quite cold enough to be good for anything, certainly not for quenching his thirst. There are no more fireflies, and it's gotten darker earlier than it did only a few days ago. They drive through town, past the green and the shops.

"Almost there," Al says mournfully.

They turn onto Chestnut Street, go half a block, then pull into the driveway. Ivan is out on the front porch, waiting for them maybe, or just getting some air. He stands up when the car pulls in. Charlie is afraid to look at his father, but he does anyway. His father looks just the same as he did when he drove Charlie to the bus, only now he's wearing a blue shirt, beige slacks, and loafers without any socks. He stands in front of the house and doesn't move; he's frozen in place. Charlie starts to open the car door before the car comes to a stop. As he walks to his father, the patch Charlie's grandmother stitched on his jacket begins to glow like a piece of ashy, forgotten meteor.

Charlie does his best not to talk to anyone for the rest of the evening, and as soon as he can, he escapes up to his room. When Amanda comes to his room, the light is off and she can't make anything out.

"Are you here?" she says.

The window is open and the white rice-paper shade moves back and forth, hitting against the sill. The children's grandfather is spending the night, and he and their mom and dad are out on the porch, drinking beer and talking low. So low, Amanda is pretty certain that they're talking about her.

"I'm here," Charlie says.

For some reason he doesn't want to take any of his clothes off before going to bed, not even his jacket. Amanda sees the phosphorescent dinosaur patch and she follows it to the bed. She sits down on the edge of the bed, and, though her eyes haven't adjusted to the dark, she can feel Charlie's presence.

"I guess you didn't get to spend a lot of time at the museum," Amanda says.

"Two hours," Charlie says.

"That patch is pretty neat," Amanda says. She can see his face now.

"How do you feel?" Charlie asks Amanda formally.

"They're all crazy," Amanda says. "I'm fine. I'm great."

"Yeah," Charlie quickly agrees.

"I wish I could have gone to New York instead of going to that disgusting hospital," Amanda says.

Amanda is the one who really should have gone to New York. She's the one who's so wild to live there.

"See anybody famous?" she asks.

She is a maniac for famous people and has already seen George Burns, James Taylor, Sting, and Carol Channing, all walking down the street, and nobody, except for Amanda, even stared at them.

"Nah," Charlie says. "It's too close to Labor Day. All the famous people go to their vacation homes."

"Mick Jagger goes to Montauk," Amanda says wistfully.

They listen to the rice-paper shade hitting against the sill.

"I wish it was the beginning of the summer," Charlie says.

They can hear their father's raised voice outside; he is arguing with someone, their mom or Grandpa Al, but they can't make out the words. They don't want to.

"Don't tell Mom," Amanda whispers. "My throat hurts."

Charlie reaches into his pocket; behind the dinosaur patch he bought for Sevrin there's a roll of Life Savers.

"Here," he says. He puts the roll of Life Savers into Amanda's hand and recoils when he feels how cold her hand is.

"You can't catch it from touching me or anything like that," Amanda tells him.

"I know," Charlie says, embarrassed. He wasn't afraid of that, he was afraid of the cold. He thinks of his tyrannosaurus walking on the icy ground as the sky fills with shooting stars. "You can keep the whole roll," he says.

Amanda takes a cherry Life Saver and pops it into her mouth. "Thanks," she says.

Since they told her, Amanda has been afraid to go to sleep, but she's always tired early. She stands up now. Her eyes have adjusted and she can see Charlie, huddled against the wall, still wearing his jeans and his jacket and his sneakers.

"I just wanted to find out how New York was," Amanda says.

Charlie reaches into his pocket and feels the edges of Sevrin's dinosaur patch.

"I got you a present," Charlie says.

"What's the joke?" Amanda says.

"No joke," Charlie tells her.

76

He moves to the side of the bed and throws his legs over, so his feet reach the floor. He hands Amanda the dinosaur patch, which glows through its cellophane.

"I'm going to put this on my gym bag," Amanda says.

"Great," Charlie says.

"Is this really for me?" Amanda says.

"I gave it to you, didn't I?" Charlie says.

"What'd you do, put poison on it?"

"Look, if you don't want it, just give it back," Charlie says.

"No way," Amanda tells him. "Thanks, beetle brain."

"You're welcome, dogface," Charlie counters.

"Just remember," Amanda says, "no backsies."

"All right, all right." Charlie kicks off his sneakers and, realizing how warm it is tonight, takes off his jacket and stretches out on his bed.

"No backsies," he agrees.

5

POLLY HAS ALWAYS taken the children shopping to Bradlee's for new clothes and school supplies, and she doesn't intend to stop now. The parking lot is a madhouse, but even before they get there Polly's so tense that her neck aches. A nervous childhood habit of hers has returned; she has begun to grind her teeth.

"Mom!" Amanda shouts, when a Volvo backing up nearly hits them.

Polly doesn't slow down. She's been cheated out of everything else, she's not about to get cheated out of the parking space she spies in the second row. She pulls in so fast that the children are jettisoned forward before being pulled back by their seatbelts.

"Good going, Mom," Charlie says from the backseat.

Polly is sweating hard. She would have killed to get this parking space. All over the lot there are mothers whose only concern is finding the right-size corduroy slacks and sweaters. Polly and Ivan have met with Ed Reardon three times this week, and he's let them know that the biggest threat to Amanda right now is

79

pneumonia. Their decision to let her go to school is a dangerous one, not for the other children but for Amanda, who could easily pick up any of the multitudes of viruses that so often sweep through classrooms. But how can they keep Amanda from the one thing she wants that she can still have? Afraid that she'll pick up a stomach virus any other kid would be free of in twenty-four hours but which might keep her in bed for weeks, do they isolate her completely? That can't be kindness.

It can't be what's best.

Last night, at supper, they talked about the gymnastics finals, which are always held in June. Not only does Amanda believe she'll be in the finals, she's certain she'll win. She is already planning her floor-exercise routine for the first meet at the end of September, practicing on the gray exercise mat down in the basement, playing her tape, Madonna's "True Blue," so often that Polly already knows the song by heart.

As they walk from the car to the store, Polly has to fight off the urge to touch Amanda. Buying Amanda new school clothes feels like signing her death warrant; what Polly would like to do is keep her daughter home and lock all the doors. She can't understand how Ivan can continue to go to the institute every day, even though they have promised to go on with their normal lives as best they can, because as far as Polly is concerned her work is over and done with. She would not spend one minute in the darkroom Ivan made out of the laundry room in the basement if that meant a minute away from Amanda. Everything that excludes Amanda is wasted time. But, of course, Polly knows she's not allowed to let anyone see that nothing but Amanda matters.

Inside Bradlee's the air conditioning is turned on high and the fluorescent lights flicker. Polly grabs a shopping cart and heads directly to Preteen Girls. Charlie, who hates new clothes, has already slunk away to the school-supplies section. Amanda begins to look through a rack of dresses, all of which seem to be purple and which, at least to Polly, look exactly the same. As Polly tosses several pairs of tights into the cart, Amanda comes over with two of the purple dresses.

"Not both," Polly says automatically.

Instantly, she regrets what she's said. What the hell difference does it make if Amanda gets both dresses?

"I need them both . . ." Amanda begins, with a whine.

"All right," Polly says quickly, before Amanda can explain. She takes the dresses, drapes them over the cart, then moves on to pajamas. She looks up to see Amanda studying her. Before Polly can roll the cart over to the next aisle, Amanda comes over and takes one of the dresses out of the cart.

"This one's not so great," Amanda says.

"Yes, it is," Polly tells her.

Polly tries to grab the dress back, but Amanda is too fast for her. Amanda returns the dress to the rack, and while she's there she meets up with someone she knows, another sixth-grader ready to be outfitted for fall. Polly watches carefully to see if somehow the difference in the girls, one sick, one well, shows. This girl, whoever she is, is not as pretty as Amanda, and when her mother tells her it's time to go she gives her mother a sour look. Then she says something that Amanda finds hysterically funny, and they both hide their faces and giggle. Some anti-mother crack, no doubt.

Polly was never taken to shops to be outfitted for school. Her mother made everything by hand, and Polly despised every stitch. The clothes Claire made were too sophisticated; when the other girls were wearing pink plaid, Polly wore a black velvet skirt with a matching cloche. She had dropped waists when crinolines were in. She wishes now that she still had those clothes, realizes that her mother had a real talent for fashion. Nothing her mother

81

made could have survived; Polly treated them all horribly, spilling ink on them, tearing hems as she undressed.

"You big careless girl!" Claire had yelled once, when she found a white satin blouse she'd finished only days before where Polly had left it, jumbled into a ball on the floor. Later, Polly had seen her mother crying as she ironed the blouse. Her mother was then the same age Polly is now. Ironing, her hair pulled back with combs, Claire had seemed so old. Polly remembers thinking how ridiculous it was for a grown-up woman to be crying in the kitchen.

While Polly is watching the girls, Charlie dumps a looseleaf notebook and a Terminator lunchbox into the cart. The crash makes Polly jump.

"Don't sneak up on me!" Polly says.

"That's Janis Carter," Charlie says of the girl Amanda's met. "She has a Great Dane that's bigger than she is. It's smarter than she is, too."

She's not smart, she's not pretty, she gives her mother sour looks. A great big careless girl who will live till she is an old woman and has great-grandchildren gathered around her.

"Go get two pairs of jeans and a sweatshirt," Polly says. "Meet us on line."

Charlie stares at her, puzzled.

Polly reaches for two packages of flowered underpants and a nightgown with purple ribbons.

"I don't know what kind to get," Charlie says.

"Amanda!" Polly calls. "We have to go."

Amanda says good-bye to her classmate and starts toward them.

"Mom," Charlie says, "I don't know what kind of jeans to get."

"Don't act like such a baby!" Polly snaps. "Get whatever you see."

Amanda has reached them. "I need a really big looseleaf," she tells Polly.

"All right," Polly says.

With the air conditioning turned up so high, Polly wonders if Amanda is shivering. Amanda leads the way down the aisle, and Polly follows. On the way to the school supplies, Amanda is waylaid in the jewelry department. Polly helps her to choose three bangle bracelets, all in different shades of purple. As she turns back to the cart, Polly sees that Charlie is still standing where she left him, in the girls' department. Polly has forgotten, this is happening to him, too. She thinks of the way he followed her everywhere when he was a toddler. The other mothers she knew used to laugh and call him her little duck. "Quack," he would call to her when he needed her at the park, and the other mothers would laugh and Polly would too, but somehow it broke her heart to know that he would soon talk, like anyone else, that he'd stop following her and clinging to her legs.

When he sees her looking at him, Charlie takes off for the boys' department, disappearing into the racks of hooded sweatshirts and windbreakers. It is much too cold in Bradlee's. Polly cannot stand it. Amanda slides bangle bracelets onto her arm, one after another. By the time they have picked up some notebooks and pens and head for the cashier, Charlie is waiting for them, with one pair of jeans that won't fit him till next September and a dark blue sweatshirt just like one he already has.

As soon as they get home, Charlie goes down to the basement. He hates his mother, and his sister. In fact, he hates everyone. He can't believe he can feel such horrible things, but he does. He doesn't plan to steal his mother's camera, but when he sees the open door of the darkroom he knows he's going to do it. The camera's a Minolta, much too expensive for Charlie to fool with. He slips it into his backpack and waits till it's quiet upstairs.

Then he goes up to the kitchen and quickly dials Sevrin, but no one answers. So Charlie goes to the pond alone, determined to get a photograph of the turtle. He realizes that no one will miss him, no one will notice he's gone. His mother is no more interested in him than she is in her camera. Maybe, just maybe, Charlie won't even bother to return it. He'll see how long it takes for Polly to discover what she's missing.

Now that Polly's given it up, Betsy Stafford has taken over photographing Laurel Smith's readings herself. The new client, the skittish one, has agreed to let her sessions be photographed, but it hasn't been working out well. When Polly took photographs you couldn't hear her footsteps; she often wore a gray cotton shirt that seemed more like a curl of fog than a piece of clothing on a human form. Betsy's presence is thick, like the murky grounds in the bottom of a coffeepot.

"Go ahead, act natural," Betsy says to the new client, but Betsy's not exactly fading into the woodwork. She curses to herself each time she uses the camera, and she's had to start and restart the tape in her cassette recorder twice. Laurel Smith can feel beads of perspiration on her forehead and at the base of her neck. It is the Friday of Labor Day weekend, and the beaches are so crowded there's an echo in the usually quiet marsh. Laurel has found a great deal of resistance in this new client. She seems overly willing to please, but there's something set about her; she's someone who believes in only one way of doing anything at all, whether it's how to store butter or how to reach a departed spirit. This is their second session, and Laurel has had no luck at all in reaching her daughter, a twenty-year-old Boston College student, lost last summer when a sailboat turned over in deep water.

Halfway through this reading, Laurel begins to lie, tentatively at first, and then, when her client leans forward, riveted, with more confidence. She closes her eyes and imagines that she's twenty again; her voice becomes breathy and higher-pitched as she describes the sunlight filtering through the clear water, through the bright white sail of the boat. As she's describing her feeling of weightlessness, Laurel opens one eye and sees Betsy watching her. Betsy's mouth is pursed; she knows Laurel is lying.

"I'm sorry," Laurel says suddenly. "I just don't see her anymore. I can't reach her."

When the new client leaves, Laurel doesn't charge her. Betsy grumbles as she packs up her equipment, and, to avoid her, Laurel goes into the kitchen to make iced coffee.

"I'd love some of whatever you're making," Betsy calls when she hears ice cubes hit against a glass.

Laurel takes down another glass and fills it with that morning's coffee. She is disgusted with herself; fakery is all over her, covering her with a layer of foul-smelling dust. She wants to take a shower. She wants to cut off all her hair with a hedge clipper and scatter it for the birds to weave into their nests. With a long silver spoon Laurel mixes cream into each drink. She can hear Betsy rattling around in the living room. Betsy soon comes into the kitchen and stands with her back against the refrigerator.

"You don't think you might be losing the knack, do you?" Betsy asks as she reaches for one of the iced coffees.

Laurel's shoulders stiffen. "It will be easier next time, when Polly's with you," she says.

She is regretting this arrangement with Betsy. The idea of a book about her made her temporarily insane, fed some part of her that wants fame and money. She wonders if she's being punished for her greed. This is not her first disastrous reading; for weeks Laurel Smith has been lying to her clients, telling them whatever they want to hear. But this is the first time she has actually spoken in a lost spirit's voice; she feels like an actress in some horrible nightmare of a play.

"Polly's not coming back," Betsy Stafford says now.

Laurel slips her sandals off so she can feel the cool linoleum. In the winter she puts down hooked rugs to keep her feet warm.

"Her daughter is terminally ill," Betsy tells Laurel. "It is truly unbelievable. She had a blood transfusion before they did any testing, and now she has AIDS."

Laurel Smith lets that sink in. She wishes she had moved the pink silk lamp Polly liked so much so it could be included in some of her photographs.

"And the worst of it is," Betsy says, "her son is my son's best friend. They've shared lunches and God knows what else. Her kid has slept in my house half the summer. They may have shared the same bed."

Laurel realizes all this means something to Betsy because Betsy is shaking. Laurel picks up the stink of fear.

"This is what I have to live with," Betsy says.

"I don't understand," Laurel Smith says, but she's afraid that she does.

"My son has been in contact with her son," Betsy says, her voice breaking.

"You're misunderstanding," Laurel Smith says. "You can't catch AIDS like a cold. You have to exchange blood or semen. You can't get it from any casual contact. Even if you live with that person, even if you're in the same family."

"Oh, really?" Betsy says savagely. "Thank you for your medical advice. For all I know, they could have cut their skins with knives and become blood brothers."

Betsy starts to cry then. She walks away, into the living room, and finishes packing up her equipment as she cries.

Laurel follows Betsy into the living room. "I think you're overreacting. I really do."

"Well, it's not your son, is it?" Betsy says. "And it's not your worry either."

After Betsy leaves, Laurel Smith sits on the wicker couch in her tiny living room and looks out at the marsh. The sunlight is so bright it hurts her eyes. Laurel realizes she needs to get out, she needs fresh air. She decides to go to the small market up the road, and Stella, the cat, follows her there. Laurel buys rye bread, a package of cheddar cheese, and three chocolate bars— Kit Kats, her favorite candy the whole time she was married and so depressed. At the last minute she asks for a box of low-tar cigarettes. She has not smoked for four years, but now, on the walk home, she takes the cellophane off the box and lights one of the cigarettes. The smell of sulfur brings tears to her eyes. She has taken the long way home, and as she passes the dirt path that leads to the pond she notices the tire tracks of a bicycle. Laurel Smith dislikes and distrusts Betsy Stafford, but she realizes that some of the stink of Betsy's fear has rubbed off on her. That is why she had a sudden urge for a cigarette, to replace that dank odor of panic with anything, even sulfur.

"Come on," Laurel says to Stella. "Don't you dare go in there."

Stella is poised near the path leading to the pond, ready to run off through the brambles and weeds so she can hunt for turtles and geese.

Laurel crouches down. She stubs out her cigarette and claps her hands, then makes the hissing sound her cat usually responds to. Stella looks over haughtily, then jumps off the bank and walks down the road, ahead of Laurel. All the way home, Laurel thinks about Polly. She thinks of Polly putting in a new roll of film and mentioning a daughter, whose name Laurel has forgotten. A dancer, she thinks she remembers Polly saying, or a gymnast.

Polly, who had never divulged anything about her personal life before, had said to Laurel, "My daughter would love your hair. She wants to grow it till it's as long as yours."

Laurel turns off the road into her driveway. Here, the ferns and maples give way to sea grass and sea lavender and reeds. The sight of the plastic lawn furniture set out on the deck makes Laurel's throat grow tight with longing. She realizes that Betsy Stafford is wrong. She has not lost the knack.

She has simply grown tired of talking with the dead.

All that weekend Charlie tries to phone Sevrin. Each time he's told that Sevrin isn't home. Charlie checks out their stomping grounds. The Pizza Hut at the edge of the common, the basketball courts behind the school, the soda fountain at the drugstore. He goes back to the pond every day, snapping photographs each time there's a ripple in the water; and he waits there for hours, but Sevrin doesn't arrive. Finally, on Sunday, Charlie phones Sevrin at suppertime and is told by his mother that he's not in. Charlie knows Sevrin never misses dinner.

"Are the newts all right?" Charlie asks, not caring if he gives their secret experiment away, but Betsy hangs up before he can find out the answer.

"She doesn't want Sevrin to see Charlie," Polly says to Ivan when they're alone. It's dusk and she can see Charlie outside, keeping an eye on the empty street in the hope that Sevrin will appear on his bike.

"That's paranoid," Ivan says. "We have better things to worry about."

They are meeting with the members of the school board tomorrow night, and they're particularly wary because the meeting was called only hours after Ivan, thinking he was doing what was best for Amanda, notified the board of Amanda's illness. This is the kind of news that travels fast, with the speed of hysteria.

"Oh, God, yes," Polly says bitterly. "We certainly do have

better things to worry about. We have enough to worry about
for the rest of our lives."

"Stop it," Ivan says to her. "Don't do this to yourself."

"That bitch," Polly says.

Ivan stirs a spoonful of sugar into his coffee. They can hear
Madonna singing "True Blue" down in the basement, where
Amanda and Jessie are practicing forward rolls. It is all Polly
can do not to run downstairs and rip the tape out of the cassette
player. She is terrified that Amanda may do something that will
hurt her; even practicing forward rolls seems too dangerous.

"That absolute bitch," Polly says of Betsy Stafford.

Ivan reaches to take Polly's hand, but she moves away as if
she'd been burned. Ivan cannot bear his loneliness, and he knows
Polly cannot bear hers much longer.

"Talk to me," he says to Polly when she starts to cry.

"There's nothing to say," Polly tells him.

She drinks her coffee, though it is cold. She can't turn to
Ivan because if she did she would have to see how hurt he is.
She can't look at Charlie, sitting out on the steps, waiting for a
friend who will never appear. She can't listen to Madonna singing
over and over again, "True love, oh baby," when she knows
that her daughter will never stand in the dark on a summer
night and, more aware of her own heart beating than of the
mosquitoes circling the porch light, lean her head upward, toward
her first kiss.

6

AS A CHILD, Polly was trained to be polite to adults. She was expected to smile at the rudest tenants in the building; she never talked back to her teachers. Being a good girl is a habit that's hard to break, so when she walks into the principal's office for the school board meeting, Polly quickly sits down between Ivan and Ed Reardon, and when anyone stares at her, she lowers her eyes. The five members of the school board already know that Polly and Ivan's daughter has AIDS, but no one offers condolences. They don't say they're sorry. They just keep looking at Polly, and, in spite of herself, Polly feels as if she is guilty of something, as if she somehow let her daughter get sick.

Linda Gleason, who has curly red hair that cannot be tamed by headbands and silver clips, has been the principal of the Cheshire School for two years. Everyone loves her, not only the teachers and the parents but the students as well. She has an enormous amount of energy, and she loves the kids, even the wild ones, who are sent regularly to her office for misbehaving. Tonight she's got a smile on her face, but her skin looks white; it seems to be drawn too tightly over her bones. She begins the meeting by introducing Ed Reardon. Most of the people in the room know Ed, he's their kids' doctor, but when he gives his short, prepared talk about AIDS, there's suddenly a chill in the room. Polly wishes she had worn a sweater, and she hopes that Amanda and Charlie are wearing warm pajamas. She worries about leaving the children home alone, but they insist they're too old for babysitters.

Linda Gleason and the superintendent of schools, a flushed-looking man named Scott Henry, go over the Massachusetts Board of Education's AIDS policy—children whose physicians deem them well enough to go to school may, others must be provided with a tutor—until a board member named Mike Shepard interrupts.

"If you're saying this child is going to continue going to school, all I can tell you is that we're going to have big troubles. Parents are not going to sit still for this."

If Polly had more courage, she would say what she's thinking. Sit still for what? My daughter dying?

Under the table, Ivan takes Polly's hand. Polly doesn't pull away, but she doesn't close her fingers around his. She wonders if Ivan remembers that Mike Shepard runs the contracting company that put a new roof on their house.

The school board members ask Ed Reardon what will happen if Amanda cuts herself and bleeds on another child; they want to know if her saliva is dangerous. Not one of them is really listening when Ed explains that siblings of children with AIDS have shared toothbrushes and not come down with the virus. They don't hear him when he insists their children are more likely to be run down by a truck in their own backyard than to contract AIDS from Amanda. Now Polly knows why she, Ivan, and Ed Reardon have all chosen to sit together on one side of the table. The accused.

"I think time will tell whether or not this little girl will be best served by having a tutor at home," Scott Henry, the superintendent, says.

That's when Polly pushes her chair away from the table and gets up. Ivan turns to her, concerned, but Polly walks out of the room without looking at him. She keeps walking until she finds the door marked GIRLS. Inside, everything is small: the basins, the toilets, the water fountains. Polly bends over one of the basins and vomits. She hears the door open behind her, but she vomits again.

"Keep your head down so you won't get dizzy," Linda Gleason says.

Linda runs water in another basin and dampens some paper towels, which she hands to Polly. Polly wipes her face. She has soiled her blouse, and as she tries to clean it off with the paper towels her hands shake.

"Damn it," Polly says.

Linda Gleason takes out a cigarette and lights it. "This is against the rules," she tells Polly. "Don't tell anyone the principal has three cigarettes a day."

Polly sits down on the rim of the basin, not caring if her skirt gets wet.

"They're afraid," Linda Gleason says. "They'll do anything to protect their children. How would you feel if your healthy child sat next to someone with AIDS in class? You'd worry that the scientists were wrong, that they'd discover the virus was much more communicable than they'd thought."

"I'd have pity on that sick child!" Polly says. "I wouldn't be afraid of a little girl!"

"You'd think about the possibilities of infection, no matter how irrational. Look, it's your child, your healthy child sitting there. You'd have to be an angel and not a mother if you didn't worry. And that's how many of the parents will feel."

Polly and Linda Gleason look at each other.

"Whose side are you on?" Polly asks.

"I'm on the side of my students," Linda Gleason says.

"I see," Polly says.

"And Amanda's one of my students."

Polly wipes her eyes with the back of her hand. "What are you, an angel or a principal?"

"Both," Linda Gleason says.

"She's staying," Polly says. "I don't care if she's the only student in the school, she's staying. I'm not going to take that away from her, too."

Linda Gleason finishes her cigarette, then runs it under the water and tosses the butt in the wastebasket. They go out of the girls' room together, and as they walk back to the administration office they pass a first-grade art board that the teacher has already decorated with pumpkins and falling leaves. Don't let it ever be October, Polly thinks to herself. Go backward, through August, July, June, May, and April. We don't care if we ever see autumn again.

By the time Linda Gleason gets home it is almost midnight. Her children, a ten-year-old named Kristy and seven-year-old Sam, have long been asleep. Her husband, Martin, is watching *The Tonight Show* in bed, trying to force himself to wait up for her.

Linda stops in the kitchen, though she can hear the hum of the TV and knows Martin's awake. Peepers, their cat, rubs against her legs when she opens the refrigerator. She finds a beer, gets out a container of chopped chicken liver, then some crackers from the bread box and throws it all onto a tray, which she carries into the bedroom.

"Hi," Martin says groggily. He sits up in bed and surveys the collection of food. "Are you pregnant?" he asks.

94

"Don't talk to me," Linda says. She sits on the edge of the bed and tears open the package of crackers.

Martin slides over next to her. "That bad?"

Linda rolls her eyes and realizes she's forgotten a knife. She scoops out some chopped liver with her finger and smears it on a cracker. Then she is revolted. It's not that she's hungry, she's sick to her stomach.

"Which kid is it?" Martin says.

"Amanda Farrell," Linda tells him. "She's going into sixth grade. Top gymnast."

Martin doesn't remember hearing Linda talk about this student before; she usually brings home stories about the ones in trouble.

"The school board's going to raise hell," Linda says. "I've got calls in to principals in Connecticut and New Jersey who've gone through this."

"You'll do the right thing," Martin says.

Linda is filled with love for him; he has such faith not only in her but in goodness. She gets up and puts the tray of food on top of the dresser. If the cat does not get to it, it will still be there for her to put away in the morning.

"What if there is no right thing to do?" she asks when she gets into bed beside him.

"You'll invent it," Martin assures her.

In the morning, when Linda goes to get the tray on her dresser, she also turns on the radio. That's how she finds out that several protesters, calling themselves the Community Action Coalition, have begun to distribute fliers warning parents of the consequences of having an AIDS patient in a public elementary school. Linda listens to the words the announcer is saying, but she's thinking that something must have gone wrong with her hearing; this happens in Florida, it happens far out in the middle of the country where people frighten more easily than they do in Morrow. Linda has always thought of herself as a peacemaker; she's walked a fine line as principal and she's done her best to make everyone happy. That will soon be impossible. Whatever decisions she makes from now on will make someone miserable, although who, Linda Gleason wonders, could possibly be more miserable than Amanda's parents when they switch on the news and discover what's out there?

Ivan reacts to the protesters the best way he knows how. He throws out the newspaper and unplugs the radio.

"Don't think about it," he tells Polly. "Don't respond to it at all."

It's Saturday, and Ivan plans to take them all out to breakfast. They always go to a coffee shop called The Station, which has great home fries and blueberry pancakes, but now Ivan says he wants to try a diner he's heard about in Gloucester, famous for its French toast. He would never admit to Polly or anyone else that he just has to get out of Morrow, at least for an hour. In Gloucester no one will know them; they'll be just one more family ordering breakfast, asking for refills of coffee and an extra order of rye toast.

Polly gets dressed, she even puts on some blush, but once the kids are out in the car she tells Ivan she has a headache. She can't go.

"Don't stay here alone," Ivan says at the door.

"I'll be fine," Polly tells him. "I'll do the laundry."

"Polly, come with us," Ivan says. He's begging her for something, and she doesn't have anything to give him.

"Oh, for God's sake!" Polly says. "Will you just go!"

He lets the screen door slam. Polly waits until she's certain he won't come back; then she goes around to every window and pulls down the shades or draws the curtains. She can't stop thinking about wasted time. She wants to scoop up all the hours teenage suicides give up and claim them for Amanda. The telephone rings, and Polly lets it go on ringing. It is probably that horrible group who want to keep Amanda out of school, or her father, who's been driving her insane. Al wants to come up with Claire for a weekend, a couple of days, maybe a few weeks. While Polly is dragging Amanda to the hospital for blood tests, Al will shoot a few baskets with Charlie; Claire will cook a stew. It's the last thing in the world Polly wants. She's always on guard when her parents visit—if she weren't she might tell them what she thought of them—and she doesn't have the energy to keep up her guard. If Claire and Al came up to stay, the children would know how bad things really are, and Polly will do just about anything to make their lives appear normal. She plans each meal for high nutritional value, carefully gauging how much Amanda eats of her lamb chop, her broccoli, her butterscotch pudding. She tells the children their rooms are a mess, when she no longer cares at all, and insists they pick up after themselves. She reminds Charlie to take out the garbage, and she always stacks the supper dishes so Amanda can load the dishwasher. But all the time she's following their daily routine, what she'd like to do is hide both of her children and build a wall of cinderblocks around them so nothing can harm them.

The phone continues to ring, and Polly looks at it, imagining that it might explode. There's no one she wants to speak to, but the ringing drives her mad. What if it's Ed Reardon? What if he's discovered that Amanda's blood sample was mismarked at the lab and it's someone else's child who has tested positive? Polly picks up the phone and knows in an instant that she's made a mistake.

Her father.

"We want to come up for a visit this week," Al says.

He acts as though they haven't been through this a dozen times before.

"Daddy," Polly says tiredly.

"Your mother can pack a suitcase, including wrapping everything in tissue paper, in ten minutes flat."

This is no idle threat, Polly has seen her mother do it.

"Absolutely not," Polly says.

"Next weekend," Al says. "We'll drive up Friday night."

"I'm going to hang up on you," Polly tells him.

"What have you got against us?" Al says. "What did we do to you that was so terrible?"

"Nothing," Polly says. "Look, I don't want Mom to be upset."

It's nowhere near the truth and Al knows it; he laughs in a peculiar, dark way. Ever since her mother took him back, Polly has not trusted Claire to be anything but weak. That's exactly what they don't need now, a weak old woman crying in their kitchen.

"She's our granddaughter," Al says. "You can't stop us from helping."

"You do what you like," Polly says tightly. "You always have."

After she hangs up on her father, Polly starts to cry. When she was a child she didn't believe in bad luck. She thought her childhood was rotten because her parents didn't love her, and she couldn't wait to get out of their clutches. She was all wrong about luck, she sees that now, and it's frightening to think what else she may have been wrong about. When her parents come to visit she knows Claire will dust the night table in the guest room and then she'll set out the framed family photographs she always carries in her suitcase. There'll be a green garbage bag filled with the tissue paper she's used to pack Al's sweaters and shoes. The children will be delighted to see their grandparents, they always are. Polly cannot believe that Al and Claire lavished one-tenth of the attention on her that they give to Amanda and Charlie, but then quite suddenly, she thinks about the velvet cloche Claire made for her. Every stitch was done by hand, small stitches no one would ever see. It took a long time to make something so perfect, longer than Polly would ever have imagined.

That night, after the children are in bed, Ivan spreads his work out on the coffee table and starts to go over his lecture. He can hear Polly cleaning up in the kitchen; he can hear the tap water running and the occasional clinking of dishes against each other. Ivan leans back against the couch and lets his arms go limp. There's no point in going over his work; all he can think about is blood and bones and antibodies. He's not going to Florida, and he'll never deliver his paper. He goes into the kitchen to tell Polly, but when he gets to the doorway he sees that she's not really rinsing off the dishes, she's just standing there, letting the water run so he'll think she's cleaning up. So he'll leave her alone. That's what she wants.

Ivan goes back through the living room; he grabs his jacket and his car keys and keeps on going, through the front door, which they never use. When he starts the Karmann-Ghia, smoke pours out of the exhaust pipe and the engine rumbles. Just above the sink, where Polly is standing, there is a window. She can see Ivan warming up the car; she could stop him if she wanted to, at least ask him where he's going to. But she doesn't, she doesn't even try.

Ivan drives out to Red Slipper Beach. Two small deer run in front of his car, and he has to brake suddenly.

He parks at the observatory alongside an old beat-up Mustang, and he rolls down his window so he can listen to the ocean. It's low tide and the odor of seaweed is strong. Ivan doesn't know if he's been avoiding his colleagues or if they've been avoiding him, but he feels as if he hasn't talked to another human being for weeks, other than the perfunctory conversations he's had with Polly, meaningless talk about the new clothes she's bought for the kids or the cost of the new shocks for the Blazer. He can see one of the graduate students, a kid named Sandy, locking up the observatory. Sandy waves at Ivan as he gets into his car and Ivan waves back. He waits for the kid to leave and then he gets out of his car and walks to the observatory. In his wallet, shoved between two twenty-dollar bills, is a phone number he's been carrying around for days. Max Lyman at the institute gave him the number. Max's cousin is a social worker who helps staff an AIDS hotline in Boston, sponsored by a gay organization Ivan's never heard of.

Everyone who enters the observatory is supposed to sign in, but tonight Ivan doesn't bother. He's not here to look at stars. He goes into the office, switches on a desk lamp, and sits down in an old leather chair he's sat in a thousand times before. The phone receiver is cold when he picks it up, as cold as a telescope feels against the corners of your eye. When a human voice answers his call, Ivan's throat is so tight that what comes out doesn't sound like any recognizable language. But the voice on the other end of the line keeps talking, telling Ivan it's all right, he doesn't have to say anything right away, he can just go on crying. The voice belongs to a man named Brian, who staffs the phone two nights a week. The odd thing is, he doesn't even sound like a stranger, and maybe that's why it gets easier and easier for Ivan to call him, so that by the following week Ivan doesn't have to look for the paper with the hotline number.

He knows it by heart.

7

AMANDA AND JESSIE always sit next to each other in class. They have been best friends for three years, and they can slip notes to each other so fast a teacher would have to have X-ray vision to catch them. On the morning of the first day of school, Jessie is already waiting when Polly drives up in front of the school. Amanda and Jessie have carefully planned their outfits; they're wearing matching polka-dot dresses identical in all ways, except that Amanda's dress has been painstakingly ironed by her Grandma Claire, up for a visit over the long Labor Day weekend.

It was not quite the disaster that Polly imagined, even though Claire, who has never believed that dishwashers do as good a job as she can, managed to wash the dishes by hand every time Polly turned her back and Al has sworn to return and fix the broken porch step. Al played endless rounds of Monopoly with Charlie and lost every game, and on Sunday he drove Amanda and Jessie to the theater at the mall and took them to see a movie their parents had forbidden them to see. On Monday evening, when her parents were getting ready to leave, Polly felt that she was being abandoned. She insisted that her parents stay for dinner, even though this meant they would hit the worst of the Labor Day traffic returning to New York. It is terrible to admit, or even to think about, but she's afraid to be alone with Ivan.

Every day he seems like more of a stranger. He disappears at odd hours, he's been avoiding going to the institute, and he has started Amanda on a strict regimen of large doses of folic acid and vitamin C. Once, while Polly was searching in his backpack for a pen, she found a folder filled with articles about alternative therapies for AIDS patients. Startled, she dropped the folder on the floor. This is not at all like Ivan, who has always put his faith in science, in medicine, in tested and proven remedies. Amanda complains about the vitamins, she says they make her gag, but Ivan insists; he gives her glasses of Gatorade and Hawaiian Punch to wash down the capsules. When Polly suggested they talk with Ed about the vitamins and the high-fiber diet Ivan's demanded they all go on, Ivan refused. What can he offer us, Ivan asked her. Nothing.

So far, five children have been registered at private schools, pulled out of Cheshire before the first day of classes. Although Linda Gleason phones Polly each time there's a parents' or teachers' meeting, Polly doesn't bother going to them; she can't waste the time better spent at home, with Amanda. She pities Linda Gleason, who has to try to keep everything under control, but she pities the principal from a distance; it's not unlike watching a puppet show.

From where she's parked, in front of the school, Polly can see two people on the sidewalk, each handing out pamphlets to parents. One of them, a woman in a blue cotton dress, looks familiar; Polly thinks her child may have been in nursery school with

Charlie. Polly is not about to let Amanda go in there alone, but as soon as Polly starts to get out of the car, Amanda has a fit.

"You can't walk in there with me," Amanda insists.

"Is there a rule against it?" Polly says. "I see parents out there."

Charlie grabs his backpack and looseleaf and takes this opportunity to escape.

"See you," he shouts, and as he gets out Amanda shoots him a dirty look.

"I'll just walk you to the door," Polly says. It is bad enough to be separated from Amanda for an entire day. Impossible to let her walk past these people leafleting against her.

"Mother!" Amanda says. "I'm in sixth grade!"

Amanda's braids are so tight Polly can see her clean scalp. The back of her neck is soft and pale. Out on the sidewalk, Jessie is waiting, shifting her weight from one foot to the other.

"I'll pick you up at three," Polly says.

"Four," Amanda says.

"Four?" Polly says.

"It's the first day of practice," Amanda explains. "I don't want you to make a big deal out of it."

Amanda leans over and kisses her good-bye, but Polly can feel her bursting to get out of the car. Amanda opens the door and runs to Jessie. When the girls reach each other, they cling together and squeal.

"My mother wanted to walk me into school," Amanda confides. She looks back and waves at Polly. Polly waves back, then forces herself to drive on.

"Oh, God," Jessie says with real feeling.

"I don't look sick, do I?" Amanda says.

"You look great," Jessie says. "Your dress looks fantastic."

103

Amanda smiles, but when they get to the door she feels scared. Scared she might throw up or something worse. She hesitates, until Jessie says, "If anyone says anything mean to you, I'll hit them."

Amanda laughs at that, especially because Jessie is so small. It's strange, but even when she laughs she feels something hot behind her eyes. Sometimes she holds her breath and tries to imagine what it's like to be dead. How would it be to leave her body behind? She has never believed in heaven, but now she wonders. Sleep, white clouds, wings. Could she actually believe in that? No, she does not. It's easier to think about becoming one with the earth. She could believe that; out of her body will come grass, roses, black-eyed Susans. She could almost believe that, if it weren't happening to her.

"Don't look behind you," Jessie Eagan says in the hallway.

Amanda peeks over her shoulder and sees a boy in their grade. Keith Davies.

"He's staring at you!" Jessie whispers loudly, excited.

"No he's not," Amanda says, but when she looks he is staring at her. He's dopy-looking, but sort of cute, too.

"Sixth grade is the best grade ever," Jessie says.

"Yeah," Amanda agrees. "Are you ready?"

"Ready," Jessie says, although as they walk into their classroom, they momentarily forget that they are sixth-graders and hold hands.

At two forty-five, Amanda and Jessie head over to the gym, their identical pink gym bags slung over their shoulders.

"Oh, no, not Charlie," Jessie says dramatically when they see him, standing in front of the gym.

Amanda is puzzled when Charlie doesn't have a fast comeback. He can usually create a nasty pun on Jessie's name in no time flat. Amanda herself is in good spirits, no one said anything awful to her, and her teacher, who Amanda thinks is too pretty and young to be a teacher, called her aside and told her that it was a pleasure to have her in class and that if she missed any time her work could be sent home to be made up. Amanda doesn't intend to miss any time. She's a little nervous about gymnastics practice, and she hopes the aching in her legs won't mess her up and push her way back in the rankings.

"Well, what is it?" she says to Charlie. She doesn't actually want to be seen talking to a third-grader. Charlie shrugs, so Amanda turns to Jessie and says, "I'll meet you in the locker room."

"All right," Jessie says, going on ahead, "but my dad's going to let you have it if you're late."

"What's wrong?" Amanda asks Charlie.

Charlie shrugs again. He has a creepy feeling in his stomach.

"Come on," Amanda says. She can hear the coach setting up in the gym. The exercise mats hit the floor, then whoosh as they're rolled out flat.

"Sevrin's not in school," Charlie says.

"So what?" Amanda says. "Call him and see if he's okay."

"He's never home when I call," Charlie says.

Amanda feels in her gym bag to make certain she hasn't forgotten her tape. She hopes the coach doesn't give her a hard time about Madonna the way he sometimes does when someone wants to set her routine to rock-and-roll.

"Well, just go on over to his house then," Amanda tells Charlie.

Charlie looks at her and blinks. He should have thought of that.

"Yeah," he says.

"Try using your brain once in a while," Amanda says. Then she runs off to the locker room. As she's hurrying, she realizes

105

two girls from the team, Sue Sherman and Evelyn Crowley, are staring at her. Amanda faces away and quickly pulls on her leotard. She wishes she were wearing a bra, but her mother thinks she's too young.

"They know you're the one to beat," Jessie Eagan says as she comes up beside Amanda.

Amanda nods and clips her hair up with a silver barrette. She had not thought about other people looking at her as if she were sick and she feels self-conscious as she walks into the gym with Jessie. She goes to the barre and does some warm-up stretches; because she hasn't practiced as much as she should have, her ligaments feel unusually tight. As she warms up, the coach starts yelling at some new girls, who are only fourth-graders, to take off their necklaces and charm bracelets.

"What do you think this is?" Jack Eagan shouts. "A fashion show?"

Amanda knows he has come up behind her and is watching her, so she bends even deeper. She's waiting for him to shout at her, but he doesn't. He could kick her off the team if he wanted to, because of her illness. She has been thinking all summer about the meet next June, because it would help rank her in junior high. For a while she thought she wanted to be ranked first in her school so she could put it in her letter to Bela Karolyi when she wrote to him to beg him to take her on as his student. She has stopped thinking about trying to get Bela to be her coach, she has stopped thinking about junior high school. She wants to win the meet at the end of the term just to win it. When Amanda can't take being stared at any longer, she turns around and faces the coach.

"What am I doing wrong?" she says.

Caught off guard, Jack Eagan laughs. "You must think I'm pretty mean," he says, and when Amanda doesn't answer, he laughs again. He leans against the walls and nods to the uneven parallel bars. "That's the most dangerous piece of equipment in the gym."

He looks at Amanda from the corner of his eye. There have been moments when he's wished that Amanda were his daughter instead of Jessie. Not that he doesn't love Jessie, he does, but Amanda is a champion. It's not just that she's good, it's that she wants to win. Badly. Enough to give the sport her all; when she's here, she's in this gym and nowhere else. He's heard about this AIDS problem from Jessie, but even if the girls weren't best friends, he'd know by now. Schools are like that, information fans out quickly. Besides, his wife, Louise, has gotten a call from some group of protesters, although Jack Eagan can't quite see what there is to protest about.

"The thing is this," he says, uncomfortable, "if you're weak or you don't feel good, I don't want you to get hurt."

"You must think I'm really stupid," Amanda says.

She has never talked to the coach this way before. In fact, she's afraid of him. She avoids him when she's at Jessie's because he yells almost as much at home as he does in the gym. Jessie and Amanda have both wondered if he just can't talk in a normal voice anymore.

"I didn't say you were stupid," Jack Eagan says. He's watching a new girl, being spotted on the balance beam. "You're a champion. Champions don't let themselves feel pain. That's why I'm worried."

Amanda looks at him hard. Her mouth is dry. In the past he has criticized her when she's messed up, but she knows she's doing a good job only when he doesn't comment at all. He has never actually said anything positive.

"Are you just being nice to me because you feel sorry for me?" Amanda says hotly.

"You know I'm not nice," Jack Eagan says.

He wonders if she would have given up gymnastics. She might have grown too heavy or too tall, she might have decided to spend her time thinking about boys and schoolwork, might have grown tired of blisters on her hands and black-and-blue marks on her thighs. She might have grown up and left this all behind, anyway.

"Thought much about your floor exercise?" he asks.

He knows he should be out on the floor, giving his usual lecture, scaring all the new girls so they'll be at practice on time. He's been accused of favoring the good gymnasts, Amanda in particular, and why the hell shouldn't he?

Amanda reaches into her gym bag and pulls out her Madonna tape. Jack Eagan squints to get a closer look. He cannot remember the last time he cried. He can't remember the last time he told his daughter he loved her.

"Oh, no!" he bellows now, so that the other girls on the floor all turn to them. "Not Madonna!"

Most of the girls in the gym start to giggle, and Amanda grins when Jack Eagan pretends to tear out what's left of his hair. Even Jessie, who's seen her father go through this routine a thousand times before, starts laughing.

"Anything but Madonna!" Jack Eagan shouts, as the team gathers around to examine Amanda's tape, making it possible for Jack to ask Amanda to go through her floor exercise first, without having anyone accuse him of favoritism.

Charlie has already begun to bicycle over to Sevrin's. He takes the shortcut, through the woods. It still feels like summer, the air is heavy and warm and the scent of damp earth is strong, but it's an illusion. Some of the maples are already turning red. The oaks and locusts seem faintly yellow wherever sunlight touches their leaves. People come to Morrow from Boston and New York at this time of year to watch the migration of geese. That's how

Charlie knows when summer's really over, when the marshes are thick with geese and their honking reverberates through backyards early in the morning and at dusk.

When he gets to Sevrin's, Charlie gets off his bike, but he doesn't go up to the house. He has raced all the way and his face is hot. He sets the bike down near a quince bush and waits, although he's not certain what he's waiting for. He just can't walk up to the door and ring the bell. He feels stupid, and he gets down on his haunches to keep his presence from being too obvious. Betsy's car is in the driveway so Charlie knows that at least someone's home. He thinks he can see Sevrin's bike, out behind the garage.

Sevrin finally comes out. From where Charlie is crouched, Sevrin looks small as he lets Felix follow him out. He turns and says something to someone through the screen door, probably his mother, who is still inside. Charlie doesn't call out, but he stands up beside the quince. He feels a certain amount of relief. At least Sevrin hasn't been sent away to prison or military school. At least he hasn't gotten some incurable disease.

Sevrin goes around to the backyard and Charlie has to squint to see him. Sevrin whistles for the golden retriever, but Felix has picked up Charlie's scent and he ignores his owner.

"Over here, Felix!" Sevrin shouts.

Charlie doesn't know why he feels so bad, why there is a lump in his throat.

Felix races toward Charlie, and Sevrin stands with one hand shading his eyes, trying to make out what it is Felix is after. Felix doesn't only wag his tail, he wags his whole body. As soon as he recognizes Charlie, he jumps up and knocks Charlie backward on his heels. Charlie laughs and pushes the dog away. Sevrin has run over and he laughs when he sees Charlie struggling with Felix.

"Get your dog off me," Charlie says.

Sevrin reaches and grabs the still-wagging Felix by his collar.

"Where've you been?" Charlie asks as he stands up. "Vacation?"

"I haven't been anywhere," Sevrin says. He's holding the dog by the collar and he looks weird. Now Charlie understands why his father complains when someone doesn't look him in the eye.

"I'm in a different school," Sevrin says.

"Oh, yeah?" Charlie says carefully.

"Actually, it's pretty neat," Sevrin says. "My cousins go there and my aunt is on the board, that's how they got me in."

"Prep school?" Charlie is becoming more and more uneasy.

"Private school," Sevrin clarifies. "My dad drops me off in Cambridge on his way downtown. After this week, I won't get home till after seven."

"You don't have to go on weekends, do you?" Charlie asks.

"It's not a prison, idiot," Sevrin says. "I might get to play on the junior soccer team."

"We can get together on Saturdays," Charlie says, relieved.

Sevrin still isn't looking at him. He lets go of the dog's collar and Felix trots off to a neighbor's yard.

"My mom doesn't want me to," Sevrin says unhappily.

"Doesn't want you to what?" Charlie says, confused.

"I can't be friends with you because of Amanda," Sevrin says.

"What did she do?" Charlie asks, more confused than ever.

"It's because she's sick," Sevrin says.

Charlie stares at his friend. "That's crazy," he says finally.

"My mother's afraid I'll get it," Sevrin says.

"That's scientifically ridiculous," Charlie says. "Where's her data that confirms that? Didn't you tell her you can't get it?"

Sevrin's still not looking at him.

"Some scientist," Charlie says, disgusted. He can feel his throat get tight, but he's not about to cry.

"My mom is really upset about this," Sevrin says. "She's not kidding on this one. She won't take no for an answer."

"Sure," Charlie says. He walks away and gets his bike.

"I'll give you half the newts if you want them," Sevrin says.

"No thanks," Charlie says.

He and Sevrin were born in the same month, February, and ever since they were three they've had their parties together. They've been planning a dinosaur party for this year; they've already ordered rubber claws and fangs from a mail-order catalogue.

"Good luck making the soccer team," Charlie says.

He knows that Sevrin's crying, but he doesn't care. He's thinking about the ride home; if you time it just right and take the bump on Ash Street at full speed your bike will go right up in the air and fly over the curb. He's a little too old for birthday parties now anyway. They're stupid. They're for kids. They're something he's not even going to think about anymore.

8

SOMETIMES, in the evenings, Laurel Smith rides past their house. She doesn't want anyone in the neighborhood to hear her, so she takes her bike, an old green Ross that once belonged to her ex-husband. The bike doesn't have a headlight; she has to pedal through the blackness of the marsh road, carefully avoiding the pitch that leads down to the steep drainage ditches filled with rainwater. In the spring the ditches are a breeding ground for dragonflies; they hover above the still water, lining the road with a shimmering band of blue. The dragonflies are gone now, but there are other things still alive in the woods. Whenever a bike goes by there's a frantic beating of wings, branches break as deer run away.

Laurel does not know what all the children in town know; there is a shortcut, a dirt path through the pines, which allows them to ride their bikes from the marsh to the outskirts of town without having to pass the graveyard. The children have been taking this shortcut for so long most of them don't even remember why they avoid this stretch of road. Some of them still get the chills just before they make the turn off into the woods. There is a sharp curve just before the graveyard, a place where the pines are especially tall; in bad weather the place is like a wind tunnel. Laurel always races her bike at this turn in the road, especially when there's a moon and she can see the iron fence in the middle of the woods. She wonders about that fence, whether it's meant to keep people out, or in.

It is dusk when Laurel stops, suddenly, as though she'd been pushed off her bike. The fence around the cemetery has turned green, and even from a distance it gives out a peculiar mossy odor, a mixture of rust and tears. There are not more than thirty headstones, and several of them have been cracked. Angels have been split in half, rain has worn away the features of little stone lambs and made them blind. There is a new cemetery on the other side of Route 16, so no one has been buried here for two hundred years, no one is remembered. It's a place where grass can't grow, where mockingbirds and crows nest in the boughs of the trees; they have plucked out so many of their feathers that in one or two of the hollows the earth looks black.

"I've got to get out of here," Laurel says out loud. Her head churns like a caldron, but she stands where she is, beside her bike. She waits for the dead, but they don't come out to greet her. They don't even whisper. Two inky feathers fall from the sky. "Say something," Laurel Smith commands, but the silence goes on, broken only by twigs cracking and wind. Laurel touches the tip of one of the iron brackets of the gate; it is sharp, it could easily cut her finger.

Darkness has fallen by the time Laurel gets back on the road, and when she finally turns onto Chestnut Street, she's certain she won't be noticed. After the blackness of the road and the woods, she's always shocked to see the white houses on this street, the globes of light behind the windows, the tubs of chrysanthe-

114

mums beside the front doors. Laurel rests her bike on the grass across the street; she can see into their kitchen window from here. Sometimes she sees them all at dinner, she can smell vegetable soup and broiled chops when the wind is right. She's checked some of the other houses on Chestnut, peered into other kitchens and living rooms. She feels giddy when she does this; she balances on the edge of window wells like a cat on a ledge. Sometimes she thinks the Farrells are just like anybody else, and it makes her feel good. She believes she knows what's going on at their table, in their beds, just because she sees them through their window, but she has no way of knowing that Amanda can barely eat and that her lack of appetite seems catching, for half of the food Polly cooks is scraped into the trash. She has never imagined that as soon as dinner is gotten through, Charlie escapes to the basement like a turtle into his shell; that Polly and Ivan can no longer kiss, that their lips seem broken and their tongues don't work; that Amanda can no longer swallow the vitamins her father gives her. She saves them in her cheek and when no one's looking spits them out, her head leaning far into the toilet.

Dinner is over and there are plates of chocolate cake on the table. Tonight the scent of coffee wafts across the street. Charlie has taken his cake downstairs and is feeding crumbs to his hamsters. He can hear his sister in the kitchen as she stomps her feet on the floor, he can feel her fury through the floorboards, as it moves through the pipes and the heat registers in a hot, cloudy swirl. It's not fair. That's what everybody thinks. That's what everybody keeps saying. Tomorrow night there is a birthday party, a sleepover, and everybody is going, but Amanda is not allowed. She has already gone to the mall with Jessie and Mrs. Eagan and bought a birthday present, six colorful plastic headbands and six matching bangle bracelets.

"You hate me," Amanda says to her parents.

She has a terrible look on her face. She pushes the plate of cake away from her, hard. The plate skitters across the table and crashes on the floor.

"We love you," Polly says. She holds herself back from crouching down and cleaning up the cake. She holds herself back all the time.

"Oh, yeah," Amanda says. "Sure. That's what you say. You have to say that."

"This is not up for discussion," Ivan says. "You can go to the party, but you can't sleep over."

"Just embarrass me in front of everybody," Amanda cries. "My life is ruined anyway."

Her words fall across the table like splinters of glass. They should be eating chocolate cake, instead they are bleeding from their souls. Ivan closes his eyes and immediately wishes he could talk to Brian; the thought startles him and then he thinks, Of course. He wants to telephone a hotline and speak to a stranger because there is no one he can talk to in this house anymore, there aren't even words to use. Amanda glares at her parents, defying them to try to comfort her.

"Amanda," Polly says. "Please."

"Please what?" Amanda fires back. "Please just die and get it over with?"

Her parents don't answer and Amanda feels the flush of triumph. She has had the last word and she's not even being sent to her room. Amanda leans back in her chair and folds her arms across her thin chest. For no reason at all she thinks of a rabbit's foot her grandpa gave her once. The rabbit's foot was white and soft and you could keep it in your pocket like a secret. Amanda loved it and kept it in her coat or under her pillow until she realized that the only way to get a rabbit's foot from a rabbit is to cut it off. She feels the same way now as she did when she hid the rabbit's foot deep in the kitchen garbage can, underneath orange peels and wet tea bags. Her arms feel spongy and something as sharp as a pin seems to be lodged behind her eyes.

Nobody tries to stop Amanda as she runs outside. The screen door slams behind her and her breathing is coming hard. It's black outside with just the first few stars high above the trees. Amanda runs into the driveway and then in a zigzag across the lawn, but when she gets to the sidewalk she stops and starts to cry. Stupid, but it was only at the dinner table that she realized in order to die of a disease you really have to die and not come back. She stands on the sidewalk with her sneakers straddling the cracks in the cement and covers her eyes with her hands.

Across the street, Laurel Smith grabs the sleeves of her cardigan and pulls the wool over her fingers. Amanda's pale hair hangs limply, like unwound silver thread in the dark. She doesn't make any noise when she cries, but her whole body shakes. After a while someone opens the back door.

"Amanda?" Polly calls in a high, frightened voice. "Honey?"

Laurel doesn't move until Amanda turns around and walks back to the house. The trees on Chestnut Street are heavy with leaves and they move with the wind and make a low, throaty noise. When the screen door slams behind Amanda, Laurel gets on her bike, pushes off hard with her feet, then swoops along the sidewalk and into the street. She pedals so hard the old bike vibrates; the air is salty and cool, but she's sweating enough that by the time she reaches the marsh her hair is wet and flattened to her head. Her sweater is damp. She lets the bike fall to the ground and goes to her deck, tripping over a lawn chair in the dark. Her breath is all jumpy, filled with strange little sobs that don't quite come out and don't stay inside either. She thinks of herself watching, peeking into other people's lives through the dark, and she's disgusted.

117

When she goes inside she rifles through the kitchen cabinet, gets a can of tunafish and eats standing up, as though she'd been starved. Then she takes down a bag of flour and some brown sugar, and by midnight she has finished a perfect fluted crust for a pie. In the morning she gets into her car and goes back to Chestnut Street. The pie is wrapped in aluminum foil and Laurel has also brought a bunch of pink mallows, marsh flowers so huge they look as if they've been grown on another planet. The apple pie is still warm, the flowers only slightly wilted. As she waits for someone to answer the door, Laurel switches the strap of her canvas pocketbook from one shoulder to the other. Being here in the daylight, Laurel feels nervous, much the way her clients react to their first séance. As she walked up to the Farrells' back door, things looked unbalanced and out of focus. She has never been at ease with people; when she was married she could never call her husband by his name, and he often complained that she never looked him full in the face but went out of her way to crouch down and greet stray cats.

It's a Saturday, so when Polly hears someone at the door, she assumes it's her parents, earlier than expected. She gave them an inch and now they're up every weekend. She has the feeling they start to watch the clock on Friday nights, so they'll be ready to jump into Al's car at dawn on Saturday. Polly takes her time, wiping down a counter before she gets the door. When she sees Laurel, Polly feels something sharp along her back, as if she were an animal with her hackles raised. Across the street, Fran Crowley balances her groceries on the fender of her hatchback so she can get a good look at Laurel; she puts one hand over her eyes to shade them, and her mouth drops into an O.

"I'm not working on the book anymore," Polly says quickly.

"Neither am I," Laurel says.

Polly hasn't opened the screen door; she's talking to Laurel through the mesh, as she would to a peddler.

"I heard that your daughter was sick, so I came to visit her," Laurel says. "I brought a pie."

"You should have waited," Polly says. "She's not dead yet."

Laurel steps backward, as if she'd been slapped. She catches the heel of her shoe on the step that needs fixing and winds up sprawled on her hands and knees. Polly quickly opens the screen door to help. She picks up the pie and lifts the foil; only one side of the crust has been bashed in. She folds the foil back over the pie tin.

"You have to watch out for that step," Polly says. "We're all so used to it, we never trip."

"You don't have to invite me inside if you don't want to," Laurel Smith says.

"I don't know why you're here," Polly says. "Why are you here?"

"I just thought most kids liked apple pie," Laurel says. "I always loved it."

The pie tin feels warm in Polly's hands.

"I'll get Amanda," Polly says.

Laurel Smith follows Polly inside; she sets the flowers down on the table while Polly calls down to the basement for Amanda.

"She's practicing gymnastics," Polly explains.

For some reason Polly feels incidental, much the way she does when Jessie comes over; she's just someone to be dealt with politely while waiting for Amanda. She has no idea where Ivan or Charlie are, only that they both left without having breakfast, each to his own private destination.

"Amanda," Polly calls again.

"I'm practicing," Amanda yells, and her voice breaks a little with the effort.

"Come on up anyway," Polly calls.

Amanda is lying about practicing; for the past two hours all she's been doing is sitting on a gray mat listening to her Madonna cassette. Today when she woke up she thought to herself, I'm not going to be in the finals, and as soon as she thought it she knew it was true. She doesn't have the strength or the stamina. Her legs have been aching, simple moves she knows by heart leave her dizzy and short of breath. Amanda pulls her knees up and hugs them to her chest. She bends her head down, and when she breathes out she can feel her warm breath on her skin. Where, she wonders, does the breath go when you die?

Laurel Smith is still standing when Amanda comes upstairs; she has not been invited to sit down. Amanda's wearing a pink T-shirt and jeans; she knows her mother has a guest, but she doesn't look at either woman. She leans up against the refrigerator and studies the floor.

"This is Laurel," Polly says. "The woman I've been photographing. She brought a pie."

Amanda looks up. "I don't eat pie," she says. "It's fattening."

Amanda is so thin Laurel can see her bones, fragile as a bird's.

"Maybe you'd like these," Laurel says. She holds out the flowers.

"Are they real?" Amanda asks. And, before she can stop herself, she adds, "They're beautiful."

"Pink is my favorite color," Laurel says.

"Mine, too," Amanda says carefully as she appraises Laurel, staring mostly at Laurel's hair, which hangs to her waist, except on each side where the hair is pulled back into an intricate French braid.

"I could teach you to do your hair like this," Laurel says.

Polly narrows her eyes; she realizes that she has read Amanda's mind just as easily as Laurel has.

"Yeah?" Amanda says.

"Would that be okay?" Laurel asks Polly.

"I'm sure you're busy," Polly says.

"No," Laurel says. "The most important thing I have to do today is buy cat food."

"You have a cat?" Amanda asks, as if this were the most fascinating piece of information she'd ever heard.

"Grandma and Grandpa are coming over," Polly says weakly.

"Not for a while," Amanda says. She looks very small, and younger than her age. "Oh, please!"

Polly and Laurel Smith look at each other.

"All right," Polly says.

Amanda runs off to get a brush and some rubber bands.

"Why are you doing this?" Polly says, suspiciously. She figures she has a right to be suspicious when a woman who communes with spirits wants to brush her daughter's hair.

"She'll look pretty with her hair braided," Laurel Smith says. "Don't you think so?"

Amanda and Laurel go out onto the porch. Through the window, Polly can see Laurel, sitting behind Amanda, brushing her hair. Polly should tell Laurel Smith to leave; they don't need any help from strangers. If one of their friends or neighbors had offered them anything at all, Polly would have taken the pie from Laurel Smith, then shut the door and put the pie in the refrigerator, behind the cartons of orange juice and milk. Instead, she watches through the window and cries.

"How long did it take you to grow your hair that long?" Amanda asks Laurel.

"The last time I cut it I was fourteen," Laurel says. Then she adds, "I can tell you use conditioner. You don't have any knots."

Amanda smiles. She's usually shy around adults, but Laurel Smith doesn't seem very much older than she is. It's as if they were both teenagers, and Amanda's glad she's not wearing her stupid Smurf T-shirt.

"Have you ever been in love with anybody?" Amanda asks Laurel.

"Not yet," Laurel Smith admits.

"Me either," Amanda says.

121

"I've been in like," Laurel Smith adds.

"I don't think that's the same," Amanda says.

"No," Laurel says. "You're right, it's not."

Laurel reaches into her pocketbook for a mirror. "Take a look," she tells Amanda.

Amanda stares at herself and smiles broadly, forgetting to keep her mouth shut so her braces won't show.

"I love it," Amanda says.

"Maybe someday you can visit me at my house," Laurel Smith says. "I know you'd like it. It's right on the marsh."

"Are you just saying that because you think I'll die before I can come over?" Amanda says.

Laurel can feel bumps rise along her arms and legs.

"That was a horrible thing for me to say," Amanda says. "I'm horrible."

Laurel and Amanda are sitting side by side now, their legs swung over the broken step.

"Sometimes I make chocolate mousse tarts with chocolate chips," Laurel Smith says. "If you want me to, I can teach you how to make them."

"All right," Amanda says. "That sounds great."

Amanda practices making French braids all weekend, and on Monday she stops in the girls' room after school to admire herself. She looks older, twelve or thirteen at least. With her comb, she catches a few stray strands above her temples and forces them back against her scalp. Two girls Amanda sincerely hates, not just because they're popular, but because they're snobs who won't speak to anyone who doesn't wear a bra and have pierced ears, come in as Amanda's fixing her hair. Everybody at Cheshire knows their names, Mindy Griffon and Lori Walker. Mindy, who's on the gymnastics team, has better leotards than anyone else, really neat ones that her grandmother sends her from Los Angeles. When Mindy sees Amanda, she grabs onto Lori's arm.

"Oh, God, it's her," Amanda hears Mindy say.

Amanda gets her gym bag and unzips it so she can put her comb away.

"Hi, Amanda," Lori says, with so much fake pity in her voice it makes Amanda want to throw up.

Amanda slings her bookbag over her shoulder, and when she turns from the mirror and begins to head for the door, Mindy and Lori both back away. Amanda knows why immediately: they're scared of her. Amanda walks to the door and goes out without looking back, but she can hear Mindy's loud whisper: "Do you think she sat on one of the toilets? I'll never, ever use them again."

Amanda walks quickly down the empty hallway. School's out, but the hallway still smells like today's lunch, pizza on English muffins. Amanda couldn't eat lunch today, and now she feels like crying. They hate her, she knows. She doesn't even blame them; she hates herself too, not all of her, just this thing that's inside her. At first, she didn't really believe it because when she looked at herself in the mirror, she looked exactly the same, just thinner. She used to tell herself all she had to do was wait and they'd find some shot or pill they could give her. Now, every night before she goes to sleep she tells herself that she's going to die. She repeats it to herself, calmly, carefully, rolling the words on her tongue.

She is never going to be one of Bela's students. She will never go to college or drive a car. She wonders if it will feel blue and watery, the way things felt when she was knocked down by a huge wave at Crane's Beach two summers ago. Sound overtaken by soundlessness. Heat replaced by cold pressure.

Amanda runs her tongue along the silver band over her teeth. "Dumbbell," she tells herself. "Dope."

She wants to make it to the last meet in June. That is all. She thinks no further than that. Practice is hard for her now.

She feels sick afterward; once, she had to leave the gym so she could lock herself into one of the toilet cubicles and throw up. At least her floor exercise hasn't suffered; she's got a great routine. Evelyn Crowley told her it's as good as anything she's seen on a music video.

"Wait up," somebody calls, but Amanda is too busy thinking about practice to hear, and she just keeps walking.

Jessie runs down the hallway to catch up with her.

"Didn't you hear me?" Jessie asks. "You're not going to believe this."

Amanda slows her pace to match Jessie's.

"My father is kicking four girls off the team," Jessie whispers.

"Oh, no, God! No!" Amanda says, excited and all ears.

"He told my mother. I wasn't supposed to hear." Jessie grins. "One of them's missed too many practices, and the others are so bad my father's afraid they'll hurt themselves. Can you believe it?"

Amanda is suddenly rigid. "Am I one of them?"

"Are you crazy?" Jessie says. "Just don't ask me for any names, because I can't tell you."

"Please!" Amanda says. She knows she can get it out of Jessie.

Jessie giggles and shakes her head no. Amanda can't tell if Jessie knows she's dying. She doesn't act as if she knows, she's never said anything, but she doesn't spend much time with her other friends anymore. Neither of them does. If they could, they'd spend all their time together, although Amanda has begun to wonder what would happen to Jessie if Amanda suddenly disappeared. The girls who are avoiding Amanda and whispering when her back is turned are also avoiding Jessie, telling each other they never much liked her anyway.

"My father would kill me if he found out I eavesdropped. He'd murder me on the spot," Jessie says.

"Just tell me one name," Amanda says.

"Helen Gates and Joyce Gorman," Jessie blurts.

"That's two!" Amanda chortles. "You might as well tell me the others."

Jessie pulls Amanda over to the wall, and they both look over their shoulders to make sure no one's around.

"Sally Tremont and Mindy Griffon."

Amanda lets out a squeal. "Oh, my God," she says.

"Mindy thinks she's so great," Jessie whispers. "Now she'll get hers. Couldn't you just die?"

Amanda looks away.

"Oh, I didn't mean that," Jessie says quickly. "I really didn't."

"That's okay," Amanda says.

They begin to walk slowly to the gym.

"You'll always be my best friend," Jessie says.

"Thanks," Amanda says.

"I really mean it," Jessie tells her. She looks closely at Amanda. "What did you do to your hair?"

"A friend of mine taught me how to do it. She's almost thirty," Amanda says nonchalantly.

"Thirty," Jessie says, impressed. "She must know a lot about hairstyles."

"Oh, tons," Amanda says. "She's not a friend like you're a friend," Amanda adds. "She's not a best friend, or anything."

Jessie smiles and, as they near the gym, she takes off her charm bracelet.

"My father hates Madonna. He told my mother that if it was anybody but you using her music, he'd confiscate the tape. He says your floor exercise is so good you could be on a high school team."

"Really?" Amanda says, delighted.

"Swear to God," Jessie says. "Play it really loud today. It will drive him crazy."

Amanda laughs and pushes open the door of the locker room, refusing to think about the ocean, about the wave that knocked her down, the silence that takes the place of sound.

Linda Gleason is still in her office when gymnastics practice is long over. She has a constant dull headache somewhere near the base of her skull. Only the initial five children have been withdrawn from school, which is not as bad as it could have been, but there are still meetings nearly every night at which Linda is supposed to calm the hysteria, which is fiercer than ever.

Linda has always been something of a workaholic, she's often still at school at suppertime, and she usually takes work home with her. She has never looked forward to the weekend more than she does now. On Saturday Martin calls her sleepyhead and brings her coffee in bed, but she's not sleeping late, she's just savoring her time alone, time when there are no visits from the superintendent of schools or from parents, panicked by the wrong-headed idea that AIDS can be spread by mosquitoes or fleas.

When she's out of bed and dressed, Linda starts right in on cleaning out the kids' closets, which are so booby-trapped a whisper can start an avalanche of clothes and toys. The job turns out to be a pleasure. Cleaning the closets allows Linda to take control of something she can really fix, unlike her little sixth-grader. Linda knows some of the teachers and parents would love to see her right now, surrounded by junk, sweating, sorting out sweaters, roller skates, and boots. It's tough for her kids to be the children of the principal sometimes, especially for her daughter, Kristy. Teachers either favor her or expect too much. Linda herself doesn't have the patience she might have if she didn't work so hard;

she spends so much time being authoritative, she tends to act that way at home, too. Right now Kristy prefers her father so obviously that it would be laughable if Linda didn't feel so left out. Linda tells herself it's because Martin, who teaches English at a junior college in Beverly, has an easier schedule than she does and can spend more time with the children; he's free to make cookies and play softball, while Linda is embroiled in budget problems or a search for a new music teacher.

He's out there with the kids, painting the fence in the front yard white, as Linda arranges what she finds in her daughter's closet into piles of garbage, laundry to be washed, and toys to be put away. After Linda fills two green plastic garbage bags, she finds a Valentine Kristy made for her years ago. A doily cut into the shape of a heart. I LOVE YOU is printed carefully, followed by a shaky exclamation point.

Linda Gleason saves the Valentine, rehangs some clothes, then goes downstairs. It's almost noon and she takes out some ham and cheese for sandwiches. She goes to the back door to call everyone in for lunch and sees that only Martin and their little boy, Sam, are painting now. Kristy is sitting on the porch steps, hunched over, her elbows on her knees. Linda goes outside and sits next to her. For the past few months she and Kristy have not had conversations; they've had accusations and interrogations.

"I did your closet," Linda says.

"Big deal," Kristy says.

"It wouldn't be a big deal if you ever put anything away," Linda snaps.

"I hate you," Kristy says. "Everybody hates you."

"Such as?" Linda Gleason says archly.

"Such as everybody in school. Dorie Kiley says it's your fault if we all die!"

"Kristy!" Linda says.

"We'll all get AIDS. No one uses the bathroom. We hold it

in until we can't stand it. Dorie pees in the bushes at recess."

"Listen to me," Linda says. "You cannot get AIDS from a toilet."

She grabs Kristy and pulls her close. Kristy, still furious, struggles, but then gives up and sits slumped beside her mother. Linda realizes now how little Kristy understands, how little all the children at school understand.

"Amanda Farrell got AIDS through a blood transfusion before blood banks were screened. You can get it only two ways now, through using needles that someone with AIDS has used, or through sex with someone who has the virus."

"So you can get it from hugging," Kristy says.

"No," Linda says. "You can't."

"You said sex!" Kristy says. "That's sex."

Martin and Sam are still working; they both have white paint in their hair. Two young women are running their Newfoundlands, who lumber past like huge, black bears. Linda can feel her daughter's thin shoulder blades through her T-shirt. She probably thinks sex means holding hands. She's a child who keeps her fears to herself, and this must be pretty bad for her to blurt it out. Linda imagines all the fourth-grade girls afraid to use the toilet, whispering as they duck behind the bushes on the playing field, rushing to pull down their underpants, afraid a teacher will catch them. It's not just Kristy who needs to know more about sex, it's all of them. Linda has always intended to tell her children the facts of life slowly, explaining first how cows and horses conceive and give birth, waiting at least until they were in junior high before she told them any details about human sexuality. It's not that she's a prude, she just thought there was plenty of time to learn those details. But that was before, before little girls began to equate holding hands and using public toilets with death.

She will call an assembly. She'll invite Ed Reardon to come; she'll find a speaker from an AIDS organization who specializes in education. She will not put this issue up for the school board to debate; their discussion of the assembly might drag on for weeks and her students need to know now what AIDS is and how they can and cannot be exposed. She will not let another week go by with those little girls too afraid to use the toilet. She will not think about whether or not the school has a right to call children into an auditorium and tell them about sex a little too soon. A little too soon is better than a little too late. And if someone calls her on the carpet and tells her she has no right to make this decision, she will simply tell them that, in this instance, they are all her children.

The letters go out on September 15. Addressed to three hundred eighty households, the letter is brief, belying the many long hours Linda Gleason has slaved over it, searching for words that will not seem threatening. Included with the letter is a permission slip each child is to deliver to his or her teacher. Some of the letters reach their destination overnight; Linda Gleason knows this because by two the following day the calls begin, and by two-thirty both secretaries in Linda's office are in tears. Linda takes the phone for a moment and feels paralyzed by the hate coming out of the receiver, something about the fiery hand of God, something about sinners and those who deserve to die. Linda hangs up the phone and wipes the palm of her hand on her skirt.

"If they're rude, hang up on them," Linda Gleason tells both secretaries.

Linda Gleason has already refused calls from the Morrow *Chronicle* and *The Boston Globe*. Now she goes into her office and locks the door so she can hastily type up a statement for the newspapers. She wonders if she has made a bad situation worse, if she has let herself in for it. She stops typing and lights a cigarette. She's shocked by the reaction to the coming assembly. This is not some rural school district where battles over sex education have been impassioned and vicious. This is Morrow, she can see the town common from her window. She can see the coffee shop where Martin takes the kids for breakfast on Sunday so she can get some extra sleep. She can also see several of her teachers in the parking lot, standing in a close circle, heads down. Linda leaves her half-written statement in the typewriter and puts out her cigarette in a coffee cup.

In the parking lot, six teachers argue. It is an awful situation, on this they can all agree. They tell each other that Linda Gleason doesn't even seem like the same person anymore. Two of them are elected to write the petition asking for Linda's resignation, and they will begin to circulate it in the morning. Linda grabs her jacket and tells the secretaries she's going over to the stationery store to buy manila envelopes. The secretaries nod, even though there's a boxful of envelopes in the supply closet.

Linda walks to the town green. At this time of day it is nearly deserted, except for a few mothers and toddlers. The old basset hound that belongs to Jack Larson, who owns the little market, is patrolling the pathways, stopping every few feet and plunking himself down so that strollers have to step over him. The broad elms that used to line the common all fell to Dutch elm disease, but the maples that have taken their place are so tall now they meet and their limbs entwine.

Linda sits down on a bench, reaches into her jacket pocket, and pulls out rubber bands, a spider ring that belongs to her son, and her cigarettes. She's going to quit today; she doesn't even enjoy it anymore, it's just a bad habit. She lights one last cigarette and smokes it slowly, then crushes it on the path and starts to walk back to school. It's easier for her to breathe now,

130

her face doesn't feel quite so hot. She doesn't think about betrayals or cruelty, she thinks about ordering next month's lunch supplies from the food service; she considers hot dogs and beans, English-muffin pizzas, Jell-O with fruit.

Two hundred sixty signed permission slips are sent back, and Linda Gleason feels some consolation when she finds out that only thirty-two teachers and parents have signed the petition against her, not enough to put her job in jeopardy, just enough to make her uncomfortable each time she walks down the halls. The Community Action Coalition people have stopped leafleting, but Linda has heard they're still holding small, solemn meetings in rec rooms and basements. A few of the members of the Coalition stand outside the school on the morning of the assembly; they mill around near the bicycle racks, and those with school-age sons and daughters hold their children by the hand, making it clear they won't allow them inside the school today.

Charlie's class is one of the first to file into the assembly hall. He has sneaked a science book under his sweater and the binding feels hard against his chest. As far as Charlie is concerned, this is just another boring assembly, only this time it's Amanda's fault that they all have to sit here and listen to a bunch of doctors. Charlie sits down on a metal chair and pulls his book out of his sweater. He starts reading right away, but it's so noisy when the older grades arrive that it's hard for him to concentrate. He dogears a page of his book—he's up to the section on butterflies and he thinks he's sighted a rare species at the pond—and when he looks up he suddenly realizes that he's flanked by empty chairs. For a moment, Charlie is confused, he wonders if he's supposed to move down a seat. He looks over at Barry Wagoner, who's one seat away. Barry quickly turns to Judd Erickson, who's sitting next to him, and they both crack up, but they seem kind of

131

nervous and weird as they're laughing and Charlie understands, all at once, that no one wants to sit next to him.

The art teacher, Miss Levy, walks past, then stops at the end of the row and motions for the boys to move down.

"Come on, guys," she says when she's ignored. "Make some space."

No one moves. Charlie feels himself getting hot; kids in his class are staring at him. Miss Levy comes up behind them and puts one hand on Barry Wagoner's shoulder.

"Let's all move down," she says.

Barry shakes his head. "I don't have to sit next to him," he says to Miss Levy. "You can't make me."

"You really are a fat, stupid slob," Charlie says to Barry.

"Charlie," Miss Levy says.

Charlie gives her the meanest look he can, even though he's always liked her, and Miss Levy kind of shrinks away from him. That's when Charlie knows she won't do anything to stop him. He gets up, pulls his chair out so he can slip into the row behind him, and heads toward the door. Miss Levy calls to him, but he just ignores her and walks out of the auditorium, past a class of fifth-graders. He goes down the hall, past classrooms, past the cafeteria, toward the front door. Something inside him is exploding with little pops of fury. He'd like to strangle Amanda. He knows this is all her fault. She's the reason why everyone was staring at him, and he didn't even do anything; she's the sick one.

No one stops him. He just walks out the door. He holds his book so tightly that his fingers hurt. He realizes he's forgotten his jacket, but he doesn't care. When he passes the playground he sees someone is out on the swings. It's Amanda and she's not really swinging, just moving back and forth slowly with her sneakers scraping against the earth. Charlie stands there watching her; even from this distance he can hear the creak of the chain as the swing moves. And then, for no reason at all, Charlie is afraid that his sister will look up and see him. He takes off, as fast as he can, and even though he feels certain he's heading in the wrong direction, he doesn't once stop until he's all the way home.

9

NEARLY EVERY NIGHT after dinner, when the children are in bed, Ivan goes back to the institute. None of his colleagues asks him any questions, they're used to what anyone else would consider odd working hours; last year there was one graduate student from California everyone called the Vampire—he worked only from nine at night until dawn, no one had ever seen him during the day. Once, Ivan walked right past him outside the hardware store, not recognizing him in the daylight.

Polly never asks Ivan where he's going. She's pulled out the pieces of a quilt she started years ago, although Ivan suspects she doesn't really work on it. Tonight Ivan makes a pot of strong coffee in the outer office, pours himself a cup, then goes into his office and locks the door. He dials the hotline and, while the phone is ringing, adds Cremora to his coffee. A man answers the phone on the second ring, but Ivan doesn't recognize the voice. He's had to wait for Brian to get off other calls before, so he's prepared to hold on. Tonight he wants to ask Brian more about interferon, a drug Brian used to go to Mexico for when he was in California last year, but tonight Brian isn't there to answer his questions. It's only when Ivan refuses to get off the phone that he's told how sick Brian's been all along. For the past few weeks he brought a canister of oxygen with him when he answered phones, and over the weekend, while Ivan was fixing the broken radiator in the living room, Brian had a recurrence of pneumocystis. He is not coming back.

Later, Polly notices that Ivan's face is puffy, he seems folded in on himself, as though he's shrunk. They've been taking turns getting up with Amanda; she's so hot at night that her sheets have to be stripped and her nightgown changed at least once before morning. Tonight it's Polly's turn, but Ivan tells her to stay in bed. He follows Amanda's voice down the hallway; she's half asleep, she always is, and in the morning she won't remember being lifted out of bed. When he changes her, pulling the flannel nightgown over her head, Ivan thinks about changing her diaper when she was a baby. He thinks about the smell of powder, the silky feel of her bare skin. Now, when he picks her up so he can strip the bed, Amanda smells bad, there's a sulfury scent on her skin. She has pink nail polish on her fingernails, but her hands don't seem much bigger than they did when she was a baby.

"All right?" Polly says when Ivan comes back.

Ivan pulls off his sweater and his slacks. He twists the buttons on his shirt heartlessly and two pop off and fall to the floor.

"I'm going into Boston tomorrow," Ivan says. "A friend of mine is dying."

Polly sits up in bed and watches him as he finishes undressing. He looks breakable to her; he's all bones. "Is it someone I know?" Polly asks.

"No," Ivan says. "But he has AIDS. Do you want to come with me?"

136

Polly stops looking at Ivan; she reaches for the clock on the night table and sets the alarm. Ivan takes off his shoes and socks last. He sits heavily on the bed; he can feel Polly turning away from him.

"I'm too tired to go anywhere," Polly says. "If you want to take flowers, you should buy them here before you leave. They'll be much more expensive in Boston."

Her voice breaks as she speaks, but other than that Polly doesn't give herself away.

"All right," Ivan says as he turns out the light. "I'll do that."

He chooses daylilies, yellow ones, even though they're three dollars a stem. The flowers are wrapped in thin green tissue paper, and when Ivan parks on Marlborough Street, they slide onto the floor of the Karmann-Ghia. This morning he talked with the supervisor of the hotline, who phoned Brian and got permission to release his address. The college students are back from summer vacation and there are U-Haul vans double-parked up and down the street. The brownstone where Brian lives is broken up into three condos. Once it was a single-family mansion; there are crimson and blue stained-glass windows just above the door, the floor of the hallway is a circular pattern of white and black marble. The building is a formidable one; lawyers live on the first and third floors. Brian spends a great deal of time looking out his window, which has black iron bars. When he watches Marlborough Street he's glad he never let the guys in his band talk him into moving to Los Angeles permanently when their first album took off. He was born in New Hampshire and he always wanted to live in Boston. He has sworn that he'll never let himself just lie in bed and watch TV, but he's started to watch game shows. He cannot bring himself to listen to records or CDs, although he dreams of music. He has a collection of songs he's written in the past few months, music far ·different from anything he ever wrote for the band; he's been composing for instruments none of them could play. Bassoon, oboe, violin. Black-and-blue music with a line of pure white fury through the middle, a line of stars, a line of desolation as cold as the moon. He's just begun to realize he's been writing dirges. He keeps them in a folder; no one will ever hear them, except for Brian, who hears the music in his mind. At night it helps him fall asleep. It helps him separate himself from his anger. No one could stay as angry as he was and survive; he would implode, ignite his clothes with a butane lighter, jump out a twelfth-story window.

He's twenty-eight years old and he wets the bed every night. He knows he will have to have a catheter soon, but he couldn't stand it if it were now. The nurse who sleeps in every night doesn't even know about this; rather than be humiliated, he stays in bed, on the urine-soaked sheets until Adelle comes in the morning to relieve the nurse. Adelle was once his biggest fan, she was the band's secretary, a gofer really, but now she works for him alone. In his will he's left her everything, including this apartment, but it isn't enough. In the beginning he made charts and lists, he was obsessed with figuring out how he got AIDS, he has been in love only with men, but he has slept with both men and women, and years ago he shot cocaine all through a tour of the South without ever thinking twice when he shared someone's needle. He's so used to thinking *I've gotta quit* every time he reaches for a cigarette he still thinks it even though there's no reason to quit anymore. He always makes certain to smoke far away from his oxygen tank; he sits by the window so the smoke spirals outward, between the bars.

Last week, before Brian had this relapse, Reggie came to visit. Reggie was so uncomfortable that Brian was doubly glad he hasn't told his family in New Hampshire. They have never approved of anything about him other than the money he's made. Reggie didn't touch anything in the apartment; he had a blank, startled look on his face, and Brian realized Reggie had never seen the welts of Kaposi's sarcoma on his face before. The band's latest record has been an enormous flop, and they have to do whatever they can to salvage their careers. Without thinking, Brian began to cry when Reggie told him they had found a new lead singer. That made Reggie back even farther away.

"Look, forget I told you," he said.

"No, really," Brian said. "I'm happy for you guys."

"Yeah?" Reggie had said. He turned away and Brian could see his body shake with a slow sob. "Man," Reggie said without ever facing Brian again. "Why did you do this to us?"

Today Adelle has brought a box of little cakes she picked up at Bildner's, and she's making a pot of tea they can have when his guest arrives. Brian will not have any of it; he has problems swallowing. Adelle makes him a mixture of spring water and honey and some kind of liquid protein. From the window, Brian can see a man enter the brownstone, and when the buzzer goes off Brian yells to Adelle, "He's here."

God, he's actually excited to have company. This guy he doesn't even know, but of course when Ivan comes in Brian realizes he does know him. He's talked to him for hours; he knows things about Ivan no one else will ever or can ever know. Before she brought him into the living room, Adelle took Ivan's jacket and said, "Let me warn you. He doesn't exactly look like his photographs right now."

"All right," Ivan said. He has never seen a photograph of Brian and what he sees now is a very thin man who has lost most of his hair. Brian wears a gold hoop in one of his earlobes, and loose blue jeans. A few months ago these jeans probably fit him just right; now Brian has to hold onto them when he stands up to greet Ivan. They shake hands and then Ivan gives Brian the flowers. Brian studies the lilies for a moment, then gives them to Adelle to put in a vase.

"I came to see you," Ivan says. He can't believe how desperate he sounds.

"Great," Brian says. "Have a seat."

Adelle goes into the kitchen for the tea; the apartment is cavernous and her footsteps echo. An entire wall in the living room is taken up by tape equipment; next to the window is a piano that Brian doesn't use anymore. The ivory is too cold; when he tries to play he feels that if he pushed a little harder his fingers would snap off at the bone.

"I guess I came to thank you," Ivan says.

Brian begins to cough, and he turns his head away. The cough shakes his whole body. Ivan grabs a box of Kleenex off the coffee table and holds it out, but Brian shakes his head. He can't cough anything up; it's all trapped inside him. Ivan feels panicky; he reaches into his pocket and finds a roll of Life Savers he bought for Charlie but forgot to give him.

"Take one of these," Ivan says. "This will do the trick."

Brian takes one of the Life Savers, but instead of eating it he holds it up to the light. "I used to love these," he says. He puts the Life Saver on the table, reaches for a cigarette, lights it, and coughs.

"I plan to quit when I'm thirty," Brian says. Ivan stares at him. "That's a joke," Brian tells him.

"Ah," Ivan says. "I'm not very good at those lately."

"No," Brian says. "Tell me about Amanda. Tell me how she is."

Ivan looks at him, uncomfortable, then he sees that Brian is sincere. He really wants to hear, and so Ivan tells him, tells him how she has taken to wearing her hair in a French braid, how she feels in his arms, so damp and thin, when he goes to her in the middle of the night. He tells him that he has tried everything for her diarrhea, but that on some days she has to miss school because of it. And then, for some reason, Ivan begins to talk about the stars. He tells Brian the stories he used to tell the children, stories of mythical heroes plucked from death and set into the sky. In every story there is a reward for bravery, for courage; in each, flesh and blood is transformed into blinding white light.

Brian has closed his eyes, and when Ivan stops talking he opens his eyes, slowly; even this takes great effort.

"Beautiful," Brian says. His voice is thick, no longer the voice of a singer. He lights another cigarette and asks, "How's Amanda's vitamin therapy going?"

"She hasn't gotten any better," Ivan says, "but then she hasn't gotten any worse."

"That's something," Brian says. "Isn't it?"

Adelle comes in with the tea and cakes.

"Put out that cigarette," she says.

"Don't give me orders," Brian says, but he stubs out the cigarette. Blue smoke hangs in the air like a spider's web. "Pour the fucking tea."

"I stay only because of his charm," Adelle tells Ivan. "Keep it up, I tell him. Good for you, you're too mean and too stubborn to die fast."

Ivan takes a sip of his tea because his throat feels so tight. What the hell is he supposed to do without Brian? Who will there be for him to talk to?

"That's right," Brian says. "And when I do I'm coming back. I'm not taking this lying down."

Adelle grins at him, but as soon as he turns away, she looks as if she might burst into tears. She's brought Brian a glass of spring water, which he drinks now. He's so pale it's almost possible to see the water through the delicate skin of his throat. Brian is tired. Ivan can see now that he has overstayed. Brian leans forward. He has extremely blue eyes; girls who fell in love with his picture could never decide if they were aqua or sapphire.

"Kids are funny," Brian says. "They can be stronger than we are. Don't give up on her."

"No," Ivan says. "I won't."

"Don't listen to doctors. They told me I'd be dead months ago."

"And here you are," Ivan says.

It's late now, and the sunlight is fading. Adelle coughs and goes to the windows to lift the shades higher. When the light fills the room, Ivan swears he can see all the bones in Brian's body rising to the surface like fish. He can see Brian dissolving, and in this instant Ivan realizes that Brian is barely here, he is already looking at something far away, something in another dimension no one else can see.

10

LAUREL SMITH sits in the bleachers with her knees pulled up, her feet balanced on the empty seat in front of her, her toes curled so her rubber flipflops won't fall off. She chose this side of the gym because it's much less crowded than the rows of bleachers she faces, where students and families are scrambling for good seats. This is the first meet of the season, and it's against Medfield, a school farther west, which is Cheshire's archrival. It's an important meet, and Laurel knows it's an honor for her to have been invited by Amanda. During the time they've spent together Laurel has been the instructor, teaching Amanda how to braid her hair, how to simmer chocolate for mousse, how to scoop sand in the marsh and find peculiar blue crabs. Now Amanda wants to show her something, and that's why Laurel's here, even though she should be at work.

Laurel was lucky to get a job in Morrow, and she knows it. With no real skills, other than the ones she's taught Amanda, now that she's given up her readings she has only the little income she gets from her parents' estate. She's lucky, too, that Marie

Pointer, who runs the gift shop, is quite deaf, so that if anyone had told her not to hire Laurel, she probably wouldn't have heard. Mrs. Pointer is extremely patient. She spent an entire afternoon teaching Laurel how to work the cash register, and another showing her how to make out invoices. Mrs. Pointer's store is not one of the better shops in town; there are no displays of local crafts, no pottery and weavings. But there are plenty of Hallmark cards, and there are ceramic figures of poodles and collies and ducks bought by children on Mother's Day, as well as rows of candy and gum, magazines, office supplies, and, up by the register, trays of cheap jewelry, mostly birthstone rings made of colored glass.

Laurel doesn't mind the job. The shop is messy and there are always boxes to be unpacked in the storeroom, trinkets to be dusted, magazines to be rearranged on the rack or, if it's a really slow day, to be read. The accomplishments of this job are meager. The high point so far has been straightening out a tangled web of ribbon. But Laurel took the job for a weekly paycheck, not for any personal satisfaction. For that, she has Amanda.

Laurel has always kept her distance from people in Morrow; her cottage is far enough out of town for her to be ignored. This is not the only place where she's felt she doesn't fit in. She's felt that all her life; she's well practiced at making herself as invisible as humanly possible. Today she's wearing a pair of sunglasses, and her hair is wound up in a knot, but she was foolish enough to wear a white cotton dress, which makes her more noticeable. Certainly Polly sees her as soon as she and Ivan come into the gym.

"I can't believe this," Polly says to Ivan. "Laurel Smith is here."

"It's a free country," Ivan says. "It's a free gym."

"Hah," Polly snorts, and Ivan wonders if she's thinking about all the meets he missed last year.

"We should go over and say hello," Ivan tells Polly.

"Absolutely not," Polly says.

"Fine," Ivan says. "I'll go."

"Don't," Polly says, and she's not kidding. She doesn't trust Laurel Smith. She's certain Laurel is after something.

Ivan was even more suspicious of Laurel than Polly was; the only way Amanda got him to drive her out to Laurel's house was to have a fit, complete with tears and threats of locking herself in the bathroom. He doesn't know what he expected, but he certainly didn't expect Laurel to be so down-to-earth. As soon as he walked into Laurel's cottage he realized it was exactly what Amanda would have chosen for herself if eleven-year-olds could have their own houses: it was all pink and yellow and wicker, with a cat who was allowed to leap onto the table and lick out mixing bowls. Ivan went to sit out in the Karmann-Ghia; occasionally he could see Amanda and Laurel through the window, mixing up something, their faces streaked with chocolate. Afterward, Amanda ran out to the car, her face shining. She carried a tray of little chocolate things, which Ivan slid into the back of the Karmann-Ghia.

"Tarts," Amanda informed him.

He didn't care if Laurel Smith was a kook if she could make Amanda look so happy over a bunch of tiny pastries.

"Look," Ivan says to Polly in the doorway of the gym, "Amanda is crazy about her."

Polly practically had to tie her parents to kitchen chairs to keep them away from this meet. She wanted today to be a special time she and Amanda and Ivan shared. Just the three of them. Now that's ruined. Polly can't help but wonder what Amanda and Laurel could possibly have to say to each other. It kills her that Amanda would rather spend time with a stranger than with her own mother. But Ivan is right, what matters is what Amanda wants, and Amanda wants Laurel Smith.

"I'll go over and get her," Polly finally says.

Ivan goes and finds them some seats while Polly crosses the gym. Laurel is in the third row. Her head is bent down; she's reading a newspaper, though Polly's sure it must be impossible to make anything out with her dark glasses on.

"You're sitting on the wrong side," Polly calls from the floor.

Laurel looks up; flustered, she lifts her glasses off.

"Everyone on this side of the gym is rooting for Medfield," Polly tells Laurel.

Laurel grimaces, then quickly makes her way down to the floor. "Stupid of me," she says.

"Why don't you sit with us?" Polly says with absolutely no warmth.

"Oh, no. I couldn't," Laurel says.

"You've already forced yourself on us, you might as well go ahead and sit with us," Polly blurts out. She turns away from Laurel, shocked by what she's said. "I'm sorry," Polly says now.

"If she didn't love you, she wouldn't need to talk to me," Laurel Smith says.

"Don't say that," Polly snaps. "Don't you dare tell me what my daughter needs."

"She's afraid to tell you the things she's thinking about," Laurel says.

"How the hell do you know what she's thinking about?" Polly says. "You don't even know her."

Polly's not about to stand here and listen to this. She starts to walk across the gym, but Laurel Smith follows her.

"She's thinking about death," Laurel says. "That's what we talk about. She doesn't want to tell you because she's afraid she'll hurt you."

Polly stops at the bottom of the home-team bleachers.

"I could never steal her away from you," Laurel says. "She can't be stolen. She's yours."

Polly can't speak, but she nods her head.

"I don't have to sit with you," Laurel says.

"Sit with us," Polly says. "Really," she says. "I want you to."

While Laurel follows Polly up the rows of bleachers to the seats Ivan has saved, Jack Eagan has to do the hardest thing he's ever done. Harder than the decision he made in college not to go on for the Olympic tryouts because he knew he wasn't good enough. There's been a lot of talk about Amanda in school, but he hasn't listened to any of it. He's something of a loner, he doesn't consider many of the teachers to be his colleagues, and he never has. The only one he really likes is Rose Traymore, the other P.E. teacher, who coaches basketball and runs the kindergarten through third-grade classes. When Linda Gleason came to his office yesterday, Jack Eagan was shocked. No one ever comes to his office, which is little more than a closet with two desks that he shares with Rose Traymore, right off the equipment room.

"You could use a coat of paint in this office," Linda Gleason had said when she walked in.

"We could use an office," Jack had told her. He was in the process of going over the new schedule for away meets and he didn't want to be bothered.

When Linda Gleason told him she wanted to talk about Amanda Farrell, Jack pulled at his hair and said, "Not that again!" And now he has to tell Amanda what the principal told him. Jack Eagan never even thinks about the blisters on his girls' hands; every gymnast has them, usually from working out on the uneven parallel bars. Because the parents of one of her teammates have a credible medical report that allows that there is a slight chance of infection to her teammates if her blisters bleed while she's on the uneven parallel bars and another girl with open blisters immediately follows her onto that piece of equipment, Amanda can no longer compete in that event. Which, in effect, means she can't compete at all, since a gymnast isn't taken seriously unless she performs every event. The medical report is rotten, but even Jack Eagan realizes there are real fears of infection involved. Amanda can continue with all her other events, but, Jack Eagan wonders, what is the point?

Eagan feels like walking out on this meet. For two cents he would get into his Pontiac and drive to the beach and go surf fishing. Instead, he asks Rose Traymore to go into the locker room and bring Amanda to his office.

She's already put chalk on her hands and she has that blank look good gymnasts have before a meet. But when the coach leans back in his chair, fumbling for words, Amanda's face loses its color, as if she knows what he's going to say before he says it.

"I'm not that sick!" she says. "I don't even look sick!"

"I know," Jack Eagan says. "I didn't say this was going to be fair. People are so dead wrong about sports, they think sports are fair, but when you think about it there are more losers than winners."

Amanda has her back to him and she's crying.

"I ought to know about losing," Eagan says. He doesn't know what he'll do if she faints, or if she gets hysterical; maybe he should stop, but he doesn't. "I did it enough when I was competing."

Amanda wipes her eyes with the back of her hand and turns back to him.

"People think reading and math are so important, but it's in a sport where you'll really learn something. You don't always win."

"No," Amanda says. Her voice is very small but she's not as pale. "The bars were always my worst event," Amanda says.

"You didn't have a worst event," Jack Eagan says.

"I don't think I could have done it anyway," Amanda admits. "I'm not strong enough. I just didn't want to tell anybody."

Jack Eagan knows that once you're committed to sports it's hard to lie about your body. You have to use what is good about it, accept your limits and work around them.

"Would it be all right if I did my floor exercise anyway?" Amanda asks. "I asked a friend to come and see me."

Jack Eagan thinks to himself that life stinks. It stinks because things are beautiful and then they're taken away.

"Sure," he says. "Do your routine."

Polly and Ivan realize something is wrong when most of the girls on the Cheshire team have completed two or three events and Amanda is still on the bench.

"Maybe she's sick," Polly whispers.

"She looks fine," Ivan says. "Eagan wouldn't have her sitting there if she was sick."

Ivan stares across the gym to where Amanda sits on the bench. Something's happened to him. He's thinking about things differently. He can no longer think the way he must to do his work at the institute; questions no longer have answers, and yet he has more questions than ever. He often finds himself thinking about the afternoon light in Brian's apartment, how it fell in bands across the polished black piano. Sometimes, for no reason at all, Ivan's throat gets so thick he can't talk. He wonders if he'll ever work again, he just doesn't seem to care, although at night he dreams of shooting stars and supernovas, and when he wakes in the morning he still sees their brilliant light.

Out on the floor, Jessie Eagan is doing her free exercise, accompanied by her cassette of "Eleanor Rigby." When she's finished, there's scattered applause. Laurel Smith doesn't know what to watch first; there are girls from Cheshire and from Medfield on the balance beam, the uneven parallel bars, the horse. Gymnastics is like a circus, with rings of events that make it difficult to watch any one competitor. Laurel Smith is reminded of a book she loved as a child in which there was a picture of a thousand fairies, all in luminous dresses, flying this way and that over a field of wheat. This is how the girls look to her, aerial and small, managing to do what should be impossible for any human body.

Amanda gets off the bench and goes to the mat. When the beat of "True Blue" echoes through the gym, Polly and Ivan lean forward. They're both afraid that Amanda will push herself and get hurt, but they're equally afraid of what failure or disappointment will do to her. Amanda stands on the edge of the gray exercise mat. Her hair is pulled back into a French braid, her arms reach into the sky. She stands there, immobile and pale. It seems that she'll be poised on the edge forever and then, just before the ninth beat of the song, as Madonna calls out "Hey!" Amanda runs out onto the mat and does a roundoff, two back handsprings, and a full twisting back layout.

Laurel Smith realizes that watching Amanda perform is like seeing a creature suddenly in the right element, like a fish who cannot move in your hand, suddenly set into a pool.

"I've had other guys," Madonna sings on the cassette. "I've looked into their eyes. But I never knew love before, till you walked through my door."

Amanda starts her next run with a standing backflip followed by a standing frontflip, then two perfect walkovers. When her routine is over, Amanda stands in the center of the mat and bows deeply. No one can tell that she's shaking. For a moment there is silence, and then Jack Eagan starts to applaud. It's startling to hear the echo of his hands clapping, even more so because he's never applauded a girl on his team before. Jessie Eagan stands up from the bench and starts to clap, and every girl on the team follows and does the same. Amanda runs off the mat, and when she gets to Jack Eagan he hugs her, lifting her up from the floor. When he lets go of her, Amanda walks to the end of the bench to meet Jessie. Jessie throws her arms around her.

"You did it!" Jessie says.

Amanda grins, then sits down on the bench, her head down between her knees so she can catch her breath. She knows this is the closest she'll ever get to a ten. From now on she'll be sitting on this bench watching her teammates compete, instead of waiting for her turn. She's had her turn. Her heart is still pounding. When Jessie gets up for her last event, Amanda sits up and wishes her good luck.

"I'll need it," Jessie whispers back.

Amanda watches Jessie leap onto the balance beam, then she looks past Jessie. High up, she can see her father and mother and Laurel Smith. Laurel pushes her sunglasses on top of her head and gives Amanda a thumbs-up sign. After the meet, Amanda is still being congratulated on her floor exercise by the other girls. She's pleased, but she goes off to her locker and gets out her clothes. Jessie comes over and sits down next to her.

"You're still the greatest," Jessie says.

Amanda is too tired to take a shower. When she pulls off her leotard her arms and legs hurt.

"My father said you could come over for dinner and stay really late," Jessie tells her.

Amanda has been thinking about Jessie a lot lately. She's been thinking about the way the other girls look at her when they're together.

"I can't," she says now.

"Why not?" Jessie says. "My mother will get us a video. I think I can talk her into renting us *The Breakfast Club*."

"I just can't," Amanda says.

She's already started spending less time with her mother. Now it's time to do the same with Jessie.

"Why not?" Jessie presses.

"I don't want to, all right!?" Amanda says. She can see how hurt Jessie looks, but she goes on. "Why don't you ask Evelyn?"

"Because I don't want to. Because she's a retard."

"Ask Sue Sherman," Amanda says.

"You don't want to be friends with me anymore," Jessie says hotly. "Now that you're friends with someone who's thirty, you don't need me."

"Don't make a big deal about it," Amanda says. "Ask someone else over."

"Drop dead," Jessie says.

Jessie goes to her locker and throws it open.

Amanda pulls on her sweater and follows Jessie. Her legs feel worse, so she sits down on the bench.

"You should have other friends," Amanda says.

Jessie ignores her and gets dressed.

"I won't be around forever," Amanda says. "You've got to start making other friends now."

Jessie stares into her open locker and starts to cry.

"I hate everyone else," Jessie says. "I only like you."

Amanda gets up and starts to walk toward the door.

"I hate everyone," Jessie screams after her, but Amanda keeps walking. Out in the foyer, her parents are waiting. Polly runs over and hugs her.

"Are you all right?" Polly whispers.

"Sure," Amanda says.

"That's great," Polly says. She looks over at Ivan.

"Beautiful routine," Ivan tells Amanda. "Unbelievable."

"Thanks, Dad," Amanda says. She hugs him, then backs away and grins. She can see Laurel Smith in her white dress waiting outside on the grass.

"I want to see what Laurel thought," Amanda says.

Polly wants to call Amanda back, but she doesn't. Amanda will always be her daughter, now and forever. That's why she can stand and watch as Amanda runs outside so quickly you'd think she was weightless, you'd think she was flying straight into the sun.

11

AMANDA HAS A FEVER again, and each day that it's lasted, Ed Reardon has stopped at the Farrells' in the morning and then again on his way home. This means he doesn't get home until the children are ready for bed. He has to leave a half-hour earlier in the morning, but he doesn't have to set his alarm. He's usually up at dawn. Lately he can't sleep, and when he does he wakes suddenly, out of nightmares he can't remember, startled rather than comforted by his familiar bedroom, by Mary beside him, and the blue blanket on their bed.

Mary has begun to ask about Amanda. When the lights are off and the children are fast asleep, she asks him if the girl's temperature has gone down, if her glands are still as swollen. Ed Reardon never goes into detail, doesn't mention, for instance, that he's monitoring Amanda so carefully and sending her every other week to Children's, where she's given pentamidine because of the threat of pneumocystis. He has the uneasy sense of betrayal when he talks to Mary in bed; he feels the same way when she's fixing coffee for him in the morning and he's watching the clock, with the knowledge that Polly's already waiting for him. It's as if Polly were his wife, not Mary, and he owed his allegiance to her. He has some idea of how a bigamist must feel, never in the right place at the right time.

Last evening, when he examined Amanda, her lungs sounded less clear. He told Polly to call if there was any change at all, and ever since he's been waiting for her call. It comes on Sunday morning while he's drinking his coffee. He can hear the kids upstairs as he reaches for the phone, he can hear Mary cracking eggs into a mixing bowl. It's Ivan who calls, and he tells Ed that Amanda is worse, she's having difficulty breathing. Ed tells Ivan he's on his way, and before he leaves he makes two calls. One to Henry Byden, a pediatrician in Ipswich who covers for him, to ask if he can take Ed's emergencies today. The other call is to Children's Hospital to make certain a room will be available. Just in case. He tells Mary he'll be home late, and he leaves quickly before the children come downstairs and start to ask for things: buttons buttoned, toast buttered. He has to get out of there before the kids register their disappointment; he has too much disappointment inside him to take much more.

When he gets to the Farrells', Ivan and the grandparents are waiting for him in the kitchen. Charlie is sitting at the table, but he's not eating breakfast. Ed does what he has to do: he smiles, he shakes hands, then he goes upstairs alone. Polly has heard him come in and she's waiting for him in the upstairs hallway. Her face is blotchy and her hair hasn't been combed. She walks toward Ed and takes his arm as soon as he reaches the top stair.

"We're going to get her through this one," Ed says.

Polly nods. She believes him. That is why Ed Reardon feels married to her. She believes him and only him, and in the face of this agony against which he is powerless, Ed momentarily believes in himself.

The bedroom is airless and dark.

"It's all right," Polly says to Amanda. "He's here."

Ed sits on the edge of Amanda's bed. He knows it's *Pneumocystis carinii* pneumonia as soon as he sees her. Amanda tries to smile at him, but she has to struggle for each breath. Before he examines Amanda, Ed slips on a pair of surgical gloves.

"For her protection," he explains to Polly, and Polly nods, satisfied, even though what Ed's told her is only partially true. He's been advised to wear gloves when he examines AIDS patients, particularly when he thinks he may have abrasions on his hands.

"Who's that?" he asks of the poster above the bed as he slips the stethoscope under Amanda's pajama top. "An escaped felon?"

"Bruce Springsteen," Amanda says. The words are liquid; it's hard for her to get them out.

"Bruce Springsteen!" Ed says. He looks at Polly, who is biting her lip, then looks back at Amanda. "Can't he afford better clothes than that? The guy must be a millionaire and everything he has on is torn."

Amanda smiles faintly as she leans back on her pillow. Ed pats her leg.

"We're going to try and fix you up over at Children's Hospital," Ed says.

Amanda nods, but Ed can see she doesn't believe him the way Polly does. She's smart, this girl, and she's tired.

Polly follows Ed out into the hallway.

"I don't want her admitted," Polly says. She has this crazy feeling that if they take Amanda to the hospital, they may never see her again.

"I wouldn't do it if it wasn't absolutely necessary," Ed says. "You believe that, don't you?"

157

Polly nods, and Ed goes downstairs to talk to Ivan and arrange to meet them at the hospital. The grandfather is gone now, to take the boy out and away from all this. The grandmother looks older than Ed had first thought. She puts a hand on Ivan's shoulder when Ed tells him Amanda has to be admitted this morning, and she says, "Go ahead. We'll be here with Charlie."

Ed Reardon gets to the hospital before they do. He meets with Ellen Shapiro, who helps get a room on the already crowded ward. All they can do here is monitor Amanda and try to keep her free of infection. When the Farrells arrive, Amanda is examined in the emergency room, then is taken up to the ward in a wheelchair, while Polly and Ivan are faced with the paperwork at the admitting desk. Ed has managed to get Amanda a private room, but Polly is shocked when she sees the sign on the door. BLOOD AND BODY FLUID PRECAUTIONS, it reads.

"No one will be wearing gloves or masks unless they have to draw blood or insert Amanda's IV," Ed tells Polly.

Polly and Ivan walk slowly, with leaden movements. When they go into her room, Amanda looks terrified. They can hear her breath rattling in her chest.

"I don't want to stay here!" Amanda says. She sits up with effort, she looks as if she might try to make a run for it, even though she's hooked up to an IV.

"I'm staying with you," Polly says. "I'm not leaving until you leave."

This calms Amanda, and she leans back, exhausted. Ivan sits on the other side of the bed and asks Amanda for a list of what she might like brought from home. Amanda begins by telling him she wants her cassette player and her own pajamas. When she's finished, Ivan repeats Amanda's list so he'll remember it: "True Blue," "Born in the U.S.A.," "Thriller." Polly goes to the window and stands with Ed Reardon. They don't talk to each other. They watch cars out in the parking lot, and after a while Ivan joins them.

"She's asleep," Ivan says.

When they go into the hallway, Ed Reardon says they can spend the night, although Amanda is so exhausted he suggests that they stay in the lounge rather than in Amanda's room, as Polly did the last time Amanda was in the hospital.

The last time was for appendicitis.

"I told her I'd bring her cassette player tomorrow," Ivan tells Ed.

"You can bring whatever she wants from home," Ed says. "We want her to be comfortable. Let's get something to eat while she's sleeping."

Ivan nods and he and Ed start to walk toward the elevator. Polly doesn't follow them, so Ivan walks back to her. She refuses to leave, she says she's not hungry, and she's in the exact same place where they left her half an hour later, when they return with a sandwich and coffee, both of which she ignores. Late in the afternoon, Ed goes to call his office and then to check in with Ellen Shapiro. While he's gone, Ivan gets a chair out of the lounge for Polly, but she won't sit down. She's on guard, she can't afford to sit down.

"You don't have to stay," Polly tells Ivan. Ivan's been up all night and one of them should be there for Charlie. It's a shock to suddenly think Charlie's name; Polly hasn't thought of him once all day.

"I don't want to leave you here alone," Ivan says.

"I'm not alone," Polly says. "I'm with Amanda."

Not long after Ivan leaves, the resident who's been monitoring Amanda comes out and tells Polly that Amanda has woken up and is asking for her. Amanda is breathing easier and she looks a little less scared. Polly sits on a hard-backed chair and reads from a gossip magazine the resident has brought them. Luckily, the magazine is filled with personal details about all of Amanda's favorite singers, and Amanda listens quietly. As she reads, Polly could swear she smells a combination of blood and sugar, but maybe it's just the scent of her own terror. No child should be as quiet as Amanda is, no little girl should look as pale. When the resident has to change Amanda's IV she slips on surgical gloves.

"I know I didn't hurt you," the resident says jokingly to Amanda. "I'm the best IV inserter in the hospital. I'm the Cyndi Lauper of IVs."

When Amanda starts to doze, the resident suggests that Polly get a pillow and blanket for herself at the desk. "There's a couch in the lounge," she tells Polly. "Go get it before someone else does. She'll be out for the night."

Polly nods and goes out, but she's already decided to spend the night in the hall outside Amanda's room. She quickly goes to the lounge to get herself a cup of coffee, and while she's at the machine she breaks into sobs. There are several parents there, trying to get some sleep while they can, so Polly covers her mouth and takes her coffee back out into the hall. Ed Reardon is there, waiting for her.

"I have to go home," Ed says.

"I know," Polly tells him.

"I don't want to," Ed says.

He goes in to check on Amanda. When he comes out, Polly realizes she hasn't called home. She doesn't want to talk to Ivan or her parents or Charlie. She doesn't have room for them.

"Take a walk with me," Ed Reardon says.

Polly shakes her head.

"She's asleep," Ed says. "Take a walk with me for ten minutes."

Polly can't remember the last good night's sleep she's had.

160

She can't recall if she's had anything to eat today or whether or not she's peed in the last ten hours. She follows Ed Reardon down the hallway; she tries not to think that every step she takes is a step away from Amanda. When they go outside the fresh air is dizzying; there is a low cover of clouds, and tonight there won't be a single star in the sky. Polly feels faint. As if he knew this, Ed Reardon puts his arm around her and guides her through the parking lot. When they get to his car, Ed opens the passenger door for Polly. As Ed gets in behind the wheel, she shifts away from him and leans her back against the door.

"Sometimes you just have to get out," Ed says.

The car is an old Volvo station wagon. In the back there are two car seats for Ed's youngest children; there is popcorn and sand on the carpet and in the cracks of the seats. Ed Reardon realizes that he should have taken their other car and left the station wagon with the children's car seats for Mary. But he wasn't thinking this morning. He's not thinking now.

"Are you all right?" he asks Polly.

"No," Polly says.

"I've been lying to you," Ed Reardon says. "I've been letting you think there were possibilities, that this wasn't terminal. I can't lie to you anymore."

If Polly could close her ears the way she closes her eyes, she would. She is having trouble breathing. She leans toward Ed Reardon and holds out her arms to him. Ed pulls Polly onto his lap and wraps his arms around her. He feels incredibly warm to Polly; she can feel the heat from beneath the blue-and-white-striped shirt he wears. She leans her face against his neck and she feels like a vampire, desperate for what he has. They stay that way, holding each other, for a long time. Other cars leave the parking lot, and in a little while it begins to rain. When Ed Reardon strokes her hair, Polly feels safe. Their breath, which is fogging up the windows, is creating its own cocoon. A grid of rain crosses the windshield and the sky has grown so dark that it might as well be midnight. What they're doing is more intimate than making love; they don't exist without each other. Polly can no longer tell where Ed Reardon's heat leaves off and hers begins. The way she feels makes Polly believe that things can be alive. She's desperate to believe in something. She falls asleep in his arms, and when she wakes up, twenty minutes later, she's panicked in the dark, she doesn't know where she is until she feels Ed holding her tighter.

"You'll feel better now," Ed tells her.

Polly kisses him and when he kisses her back she can tell he's been waiting for her. She kisses him as if she would die without him. This is the kiss Amanda will never have. Polly doesn't want to stop, she wants never to stop, but she knows she has to. She slides over to her own seat, feels in her pocket for a tissue, then blows her nose.

"Temporary insanity," she says. It's supposed to be a joke.

Ed Reardon looks straight ahead. "Not insanity," he says.

Polly looks at him and feels her desire for him all over again. She takes his hand, then lets go.

"I'm going in," she says.

"I'll go with you," Ed says.

"Go home and get some sleep," Polly tells him. "We need you too much for you to be tired."

She gets out of the car, knowing Ed is watching her, just in case she turns back. She continues to feel their kiss; a heat lingers in her mouth and deep inside her. Much later, as she sits beside Amanda while she sleeps, Polly can still feel the heat. It's so pure that when she leans down and kisses Amanda's forehead, the heat is transferred to her daughter, exactly where it belongs.

12

AFTER HE LEAVES the hospital, Ivan gets onto Storrow Drive, heading west to 93, but when he gets to the Copley exit he turns off and drives to Marlborough Street. It isn't Adelle who answers his ring on the intercom but the night nurse, who tells him that Brian is sleeping and can't be disturbed. And yet, Ivan feels good just walking in the dark down Marlborough Street, where the old streetlights barely cast a shadow. It is good to think of Brian sleeping, dreaming of something other than pain. Just before he reaches his parked car, Ivan looks up, past the black roofs; it's a relief to see familiar stars. But as he watches, the clouds move in, they close up the sky. Ivan can smell the rain before it comes, he can feel the dampness in the pit of his stomach. He can't allow himself to think about his daughter in the hospital, he won't think about the strain of each of her breaths, the rattling sound of each gasp. He just drives, and he thinks about stars all the way home. He gets it into his head that he should buy Brian a telescope, a small one they could set up at the window. He has a frantic desire to get the telescope right now; he'd do anything to escape walking past Amanda's empty room, but he just keeps driving, and before he knows it he's reached Morrow. He hasn't paid any attention to where he's been going, but he's home anyway, and it's not really as if he ever had a choice.

In the morning, Ivan collects the few belongings Amanda's asked for and packs them into her gym bag. He can hear Al and Claire and Charlie having breakfast down in the kitchen, but he doesn't have the stomach for food. They can hear him too, rummaging through the drawers in Amanda's room, going through her box of cassettes.

"You still make the best coffee I ever had," Al says to his wife.

"Now I know you're a liar," Claire says. "I couldn't find any filters. It's instant. You hate instant."

They are both watching Charlie for his reaction as they tease each other.

"Did you hear that, boy?" Al asks Charlie. "She set out to trick me, didn't she?"

Charlie looks at his grandfather blankly. "I guess so," he says.

It seems to Al that everyone has forgotten that Charlie exists. When Ivan came home from the hospital he didn't talk to anyone. He sat out on the porch, then went upstairs to bed before ten.

"I'll drive you to school," Al tells Charlie.

"That's okay," Charlie says. "I'll take my bike."

"Does your mother allow you to do that?" Claire asks.

"Sure," Charlie says.

He gets his books and goes to the door.

"Don't you say anything?" Al asks him.

Charlie stops at the door. He's wearing the same clothes he wore yesterday, a pair of faded jeans and a long-sleeved T-shirt on which a dinosaur rides a skateboard. He slept in the T-shirt and the fabric is a mass of wrinkles. Polly has forgotten to do the laundry, and there's not one clean thing in Charlie's bureau that fits him. Even though his grandmother plans to do the wash that afternoon, Charlie hates his mother for not doing the laundry. For some reason he's afraid he'll never see her again.

"How about a good-bye?" Al says. "How about a see-you-later-alligator?"

"See you," Charlie says as he slips out the door.

Al finishes his coffee, cursing to himself.

"Don't say anything," Claire warns him. "Don't tell Polly and Ivan how to run their family. Don't say a word."

"If you can't tell your own children what to do, who can you tell?" Al says, indignant.

"Anyone else," Claire advises him.

The kitchen has already been cleaned up from breakfast when Ivan comes down.

"I'll be back this afternoon," Ivan tells his in-laws. "Six at the latest. Tell Charlie I should be home by suppertime."

"Tell him yourself," Al says.

"What?" Ivan says, figuring he's misread his father-in-law's hostility.

"You heard me," Al says. "You tell him. It'll be the first time you've spoken to him in two days."

"What the hell is that supposed to mean?" Ivan says.

"Don't listen to him," Claire tells Ivan. "Go on to the hospital."

"You've got two children," Al says. "In case you've forgotten."

"Charlie knows we have to take care of Amanda first," Ivan says. "You're the one who's too stupid and selfish to understand. Polly's always said that about you, and like an idiot I defended you."

"Well, she was right," Al says. "I was selfish. I left my family and they took me back, and I've been paying for it ever since. Haven't I?" he says to Claire.

"You fool," Claire says. "This isn't the time."

165

"I'm an old man, and I may be stupid, but there's one thing I know," Al tells Ivan. "Don't you dare forget about that boy."

Ivan shakes his head, disgusted. He grabs Amanda's gym bag, gets his keys from the counter, and goes out, slamming the door behind him. It takes a while for the Karmann-Ghia to start and when it does the engine sounds like a motorboat. He makes the turn onto Ash, still furious with Al. It's easy for Al to give advice; he's so free with it, it must be. The last time Al was on his case was when he heard the conference Ivan was supposed to go to was in Orlando. Why didn't Ivan take the kids with him so they could go to Disney World? And in fact, several of the astronomers he knows took their families with them, made a vacation out of the trip. Ivan had thought the kids were too old for Disney World, he forgets how young they are sometimes because they're both so much more sophisticated than he was at their age. If he had to name what is important to him in his life he could do it in three words: Polly, Amanda, Charlie. He guns the motor of the Karmann-Ghia, knowing that he's lying to himself. There's something else he loves: science. He didn't want to take Charlie to Disney World because of science, he didn't want his son to be sidetracked by pretense: fake submarines and plastic sea monsters and talking stuffed bears.

Ivan wants everything that seems marvelous to Charlie to be pure science, the way it was for him growing up. This is the gift he's given to Charlie, it's a gift Charlie was ready for, wanted, delighted in. They've communicated with lightning bugs in bottles rather than words, constellations sighted instead of what they feel inside. Ivan has always stressed how much there is to marvel at, whether it was a colony of ants they'd found or a rare mushroom. Now what is he supposed to tell Charlie? Is it marvelous that an entire immune system can be attacked by a single virus? Do egrets and ants and shooting stars make up for that?

Ivan goes straight where he should turn if he's getting onto

93. He guns the motor again and rolls down his window. He keeps an eye on the bike path that runs parallel to the road, separated from traffic by a strip of grass. Lots of kids bike this way to school, but Ivan finally spots Charlie on his black Raleigh, his books tied to the back of the bike, looseleaf paper flapping out of his notebook as he pedals.

Ivan honks the horn, and Charlie turns to look. Ivan slows the Karmann-Ghia to the pace of the bike, then pulls over and parks on the grass. Charlie rides over and grabs on to the roof of the car to steady his bike.

"I didn't get to say good-bye to you," Ivan says.

"Yeah, well, I'm going to be late," Charlie says.

"Five minutes won't kill you," Ivan says. "I'll write you a late note."

Charlie gets off his bike and lays it on the grass, then sits beside it. He doesn't move when Ivan comes and sits down beside him, but he feels trapped. He keeps one hand on the cool metal frame of his bike.

"Great shirt," Ivan says.

"It's old," Charlie tells him.

"Oh," Ivan says. "I guess I haven't seen it before."

They're less than a foot from the bike path, and every once in a while a kid passes by and there's a breeze from the turning wheels.

"I know you're worried about Amanda," Ivan says. "They'll find a cure. All they need is time and money."

"What makes you so sure?" Charlie says. "You don't know for certain."

"Polio," Ivan says. "Tuberculosis. Influenza. Diphtheria. Scarlet fever. All of them were once critical or terminal."

Charlie is staring up at the sky. "Will they find it in time for Amanda?" he asks.

It's easy for Ivan to forget that Charlie is eight years old. He rides his bike so wildly, searching out bumps, his sneakers and jeans are so filthy, he chews gum as loudly as a teenager. He has been alive for only eight years. Not long ago he slept with a stuffed dog called Nova. In nature, Ivan knows, anything is possible. Logic is a human assumption, twisted to fit any shape a man wants. Is it any more logical for a child to die than for a bug to walk on water?

"It's very unlikely," Ivan says.

"Just tell me yes or no!" Charlie shouts.

"No," Ivan says. "It won't be in time for Amanda."

Charlie runs his hand over the wheel of his bike and it begins to move in a slow, silver circle.

"Then I wish she would just die," Charlie says.

Charlie expects his father to slap him, but Ivan joins him in looking up at the sky. Ivan is thinking about the night Amanda was born, how fragile she seemed and how tough she actually was.

"Is there anything that has a lifespan of one day?" Charlie asks.

"A mayfly," Ivan tells him. "Genus *Ephemera*."

For an instant, when he looks at Charlie, Ivan imagines he's seeing Brian. They both sit hunched over, they're both so young.

"Let me write that note for you," Ivan says.

Charlie nods and rips a piece of paper out of his notebook. His throat feels tight. He doesn't want his father to go. A car speeds by and the sudden noise and vibration make Charlie's heart beat faster. Last night he dreamed he was the tyrannosaurus again, and every once in a while the panic of his dream comes back to him, even here in broad daylight, beside his father.

Last night he was alone on earth, or at least there was nothing else like him, just turtles with shells too hard to crack and small, running things he couldn't catch. He tried to eat dirt, just to fill up his stomach, but the ground would not move. It was black ice.

He is the last of the things like him, so he doesn't bother to run and hide when the sky explodes with thunder, with a thousand fires that will not die but that can't bring back the heat he needs. He has a terrible urge to see the thing that is like him but bigger; if he doesn't see anything like himself, he knows there will soon be an end to him. He makes a noise, a bellow loud enough to shake the earth, but no other living thing will ever hear it. He walks as fast as he can, almost runs, when he sees water, a shallow swampy pool that has not yet frozen solid. He bends to the water, he throws himself at it, clawing for fish, for creatures without shells, but everything is fast and small enough to get past him or else it is frozen and dead.

He is the tyrant lizard who sinks into the water. His body is limp, his tail embedded in the cold mud, turning to clay, turning him into clay. Above him, the sky no longer looks familiar, so the tyrant lizard closes his eyes. He lets himself stop breathing. Who will remember him and who will find him is not his concern. Bubbles of air escape from his nostrils and ripple the shallow water. He lurches and tries to get to his feet. He makes that bellowing sound again. He is the last of his kind, and that is a battle in itself. Already, creatures that will outlast him, fish and turtles and things with wings, are circling him, waiting to take pieces of him, snapped off in their beaks. With amazing effort, he rises to his feet, and after that effort he has won, he can let himself go, down where there were once reeds and warm water, where there is the mud that will preserve him, or parts of him, at least, although nothing can preserve the sound he made the last time he looked at the sky.

Charlie can't tell his father about his dream. It's stupid to have nightmares at his age, to think you're a creature you've never even seen. All the same, he's glad that his father's here beside him on the bike path.

"Come on," Ivan says. "I'll give you a ride to school."

"Nah," Charlie says. "I've got my bike."

Charlie gets up and Ivan reaches out his arm so Charlie can imagine he's dragging his father to his feet. Ivan doesn't pull himself up the way he usually does and he's surprised by how strong Charlie is.

"Are you all right?" Ivan asks.

"Sure," Charlie says.

"You want to go to the hospital with me?" Ivan asks. He's not sure how much Charlie can take, but he doesn't want to shut him out.

Charlie shakes his head no. "I'd better get to school," he says. He's already decided that he'll bicycle home fast after school, tear off these filthy clothes, and put on some of the clean ones his grandmother will have washed.

"You're sure you're all right?" Ivan says.

"Go on," Charlie tells him. "Mom's probably waiting for you."

Ivan picks up Charlie's bike and rights it. What he wouldn't have given to have a bike like this one when he was a kid. He wishes he could ride along with Charlie, maybe not to school but out toward the beach. He wishes he were eight years old and could pedal faster than anyone in the neighborhood. He wouldn't know any more than Charlie then. He wouldn't be expected to.

13

AL HAS TO GO back to work in New York, but Claire stays on for the rest of the week. Every day she fixes carefully prepared trays to take up to Amanda. And when Amanda finally is able to return to school, Claire stays on, and the oddest thing of all is that sometimes Polly is glad that her mother's there. Not that she wants to talk to Claire. She's uncomfortable when they're together, she doesn't know what to say. But when she smells the leek and cabbage soup her mother's cooking, Polly feels like crying. She wants to be in the kitchen with her mother; after all these years, she wants to be close to her.

It's only the middle of October, but already it's getting cold. In the fields surrounding Morrow there are pumpkins and stalks of drying corn; there are red and yellow leaves in the gutters of the houses and on the brick walks, and some mornings when Polly takes the garbage out she can blow and see her breath in the air. This used to be her favorite time of year; she used to wonder how people could live in California without mourning for the colors of fall. Now the black trees with their rich ruby-colored leaves seem heartless and gaudy. It's getting colder, that's all she knows. Before they turn around it will be winter.

Claire has been outside, waiting for Al to arrive. Last weekend he fixed the porch step, and now, as soon as he gets out of the car he starts to search for the rake. He has a method of raking that involves making separate piles of leaves all over the lawn. Polly and Ivan watch him from the kitchen; all the piles of leaves are the same size.

"A compulsive fix-it man," Ivan says to Polly.

"Don't offer to help him," Polly says. "You'd never get it right."

Inside the house, it's quiet. Laurel Smith has been by to pick up Amanda and take her to a record store at the mall. Claire comes in briefly to get the laundry basket and goes back out to hang the wash on the line, even though there's a perfectly good dryer in the basement. Charlie is still in bed; he was up late last night, watching TV long past his bedtime. Ivan and Polly feel self-conscious having breakfast alone together. When they were first married and living in Cambridge, they always had breakfast together before Ivan walked over to his classes at MIT and Polly took the bus to Harvard Square, where she worked in the print department of the Coop. Ivan always got up first; he made extremely strong coffee, so bitter many of their friends refused to drink it. Polly liked to sit at the table in her nightgown and watch Ivan cook. Everything he did was fascinating, even the way he buttered toast. They were greedy for each other on weekends. They avoided their friends, not just because they wanted to make love but because no one else was as interesting to them as they were to each other.

"How about a cheese omelet?" Ivan asks.

"Great," Polly says. "Thanks."

Ivan beats eggs in a bowl they received as a wedding present, although they no longer remember from whom.

"My father should have lived someplace where he could have had a lawn," Polly says.

"Why?" Ivan asks as he searches the refrigerator for cheddar cheese. "He probably would have cemented it over. Neater that way."

Polly laughs. "You're right."

Ivan holds up a chunk of cheese dotted with green mold. "When is this from?" he teases Polly. "Nineteen thirty-four?"

"Mold is good for you," Polly tells him.

"Oh, really?" Ivan says. "Why don't we let your mother examine this? Let's get her opinion on people who store moldy food."

"Don't you dare!" Polly grins as she goes over to Ivan and tries to get the package of cheese away from him.

"I'll bet your mother cleans out the whole refrigerator when she sees this," Ivan says.

He's holding the cheese in one hand way up over his head. He keeps Polly away with his free hand.

"Over my dead body she will," Polly says. "Give me that!"

Polly jumps up and manages to get the cheese, then she collapses against Ivan, laughing. "You creep."

"How about scrambled eggs instead of an omelet?" Ivan says.

Polly's still trying to catch her breath. She nods her head. "You always made the best scrambled eggs."

"If you like burned food," Ivan says.

"Which I do," Polly tells him.

They're standing close together, their shoulders touching.

"Exactly why I married you," Ivan says.

Polly feels embarrassed; being in love seems an illicit thing, it's not for them but for people who aren't afraid of fevers, who don't shudder in the dark.

"The TV was still hot when I woke up this morning," Ivan says.

"David Letterman." Polly nods. A show Charlie's not allowed to watch.

"Now he gets to sleep past ten," Ivan says. "He's not supposed to do that until he's a teenager."

"I'll get him," Polly says.

"That's it, wake him up," Ivan agrees. "He's certainly done it to us enough times."

Polly goes upstairs. Through a hall window she can see her mother, down in the yard, hanging Ivan's shirts on the line. There are still some purple asters along the fence, and, near the back door, a few October roses.

"Time for breakfast," Polly says as she knocks on Charlie's door. She opens the door before Charlie can answer, then makes her way in the dark over the sneakers and socks and comic books on the floor. She snaps the shade up and opens the window. The smell of sneakers is strong in this room, and it's mixed with the scent of cedar from a bag of wood chips Charlie's supposed to keep downstairs, near his hamster cages.

It feels like any other day, a normal day they might have had before August. For a moment, Polly allows herself to feel lucky. Her daughter is out at the mall buying cassettes, her husband is in the kitchen making breakfast, her parents are far enough away from the house so they can't actually bother her. Polly smiles when she sees Charlie snuggle down under his quilt, but she goes over and pulls the quilt off him.

"This is what you get for staying up late," Polly says.

Charlie reaches for the quilt and pulls it back over him. "I don't want to get up," he says. "It's too cold in here."

Polly has begun to pick up some of the dirty clothes scattered on the floor. Now she dumps the pile she's collected on the top of Charlie's bureau. She goes over to the bed and leans down so she can touch Charlie's forehead. He rolls away, but Polly can already tell. He has a fever. A bad one. Polly runs out to the bathroom and gets the thermometer down from the medicine cabinet. She sees the toothbrushes hanging from their rack and immediately thinks of what Ed Reardon said at the school board meeting. There have been siblings who used each other's toothbrushes without contracting AIDS. Polly runs back to Charlie's room and makes him sit up and open his mouth so she can take his temperature. His pajamas are soaked with sweat.

"Oh, shit," Polly says.

She feels behind Charlie's ears and along his neck. His glands are swollen. When she takes the thermometer out of his mouth it reads 102. She helps Charlie lie back down, covers him with a second blanket, then runs to the stairs.

"Ivan," she calls.

"Breakfast," Ivan shouts from the kitchen.

"Ivan!" Polly screams.

Ivan runs from the kitchen to the bottom of the stairs, a spatula in his hand.

"Charlie's sick," Polly says.

Ivan takes one look at her, then runs up the stairs. He goes past her, into Charlie's room. Polly follows him so closely she bumps into him when he stops.

"Are you okay?" Ivan says to Charlie.

"I'm sick," Charlie says.

"I'll get you some Tylenol," Ivan tells him.

Polly follows Ivan back into the hallway and grabs him.

"He's got it," Polly says.

"Don't be ridiculous," Ivan says. He goes into the bathroom and gets the Children's Tylenol. Polly comes up behind him as he bends over the sink to fill a paper cup with water.

175

"He's got it," Polly says. Her voice breaks and she grabs Ivan so hard the paper cup falls into the sink. "He got it from her."

Polly sits down on the toilet and begins to wail. Ivan closes the bathroom door and sits down across from her, on the rim of the tub.

"He has a cold," Ivan says.

"It's just the way she was!" Polly cries.

"Stop it," Ivan says. "Do you want him to hear you?"

"I should have sent him away," Polly says. "Oh, God. I should have made him stay in New York."

"For Christ's sake!" Ivan says. "He has a fucking cold! He has the flu! What should we have done? Put Amanda in quarantine? You sound like all the rest of them."

Polly looks up at him, riveted.

He's right.

She gets up and wipes her face with a towel, then goes into their bedroom. Her hands are shaking as she dials Ed Reardon. He tells her not to worry, he'll be over in five minutes or less. Polly hangs up the phone. Then, afraid to go into Charlie's room and let him see how scared she is, she stands in the hallway. Ivan has gone down to the kitchen. Now he returns with a tall glass of orange juice and some damp dishtowels to help cool Charlie off.

"Go downstairs," he tells Polly. "Relax. Eat your burned eggs."

Polly tries to laugh but her voice cracks in half.

"Your mother's in the kitchen all by herself. She knows something's up."

"God," Polly says. "I can't talk to her."

It takes Ed Reardon four and a half minutes to get there. He's wearing old jeans and a gray sweater; he's been out in his yard all morning, raking with the kids. This time Mary blew up; they're expected at her sister's for lunch, and if Ed's not back by then, they're leaving without him.

"He has all the same symptoms," Polly whispers to Ed in the hallway.

"The flu's going around," Ed says. "Everyone I saw yesterday had it. Is he under 103?"

Polly nods. Ed puts his arm around her for a moment, then goes into Charlie's room.

"Trying to get out of raking the lawn?" Polly hears Ed say to Charlie.

When Ed starts to examine Charlie, Ivan comes out. Polly is sitting in the hall, her back against the wall.

"You're making it worse for yourself," Ivan says. "Go downstairs."

Polly doesn't answer him.

"Or will you only do what he tells you to do?" Ivan says with real bitterness.

"I'm not going to respond to that," Polly says.

Ivan sinks down next to her on the floor.

"Don't do this," he says.

"What am I doing wrong now?" Polly says.

"You're breaking us up," Ivan says.

Polly looks at the floor. "I'm not doing it," she says. "It's just happening."

"No," Ivan tells her. "It doesn't just happen. You have to help it along. You have to give up on it."

As soon as Ed Reardon comes out of Charlie's room, Ivan and Polly both get to their feet.

"The flu," Ed says. "I'm going to run an AIDS test just for everyone's peace of mind."

"Meaning I'm crazy," Polly says.

"Anyone would have had the same reaction," Ed says. "I see these symptoms every day in kids, I have for years, only now the first thing I think is AIDS. It's on our minds. You did the right thing to call me. I'm going to send a blood sample to the lab and try to rush them. I want you to know I'm a hundred percent certain it'll turn up negative."

Polly nods, comforted. Before they go downstairs, Ed says, "I don't want Amanda sleeping here tonight. I don't want her exposed to the flu. I don't want to risk another bout with pneumonia. Don't get her worried. Act as if it's a treat for her to spend the weekend with a friend. If there's no one you trust for her to stay with, I'd just as soon have her in the hospital as here."

Claire and Al are in the kitchen, rattled by the doctor's presence.

"What the hell is going on?" Al asks.

"The flu," Ed says. "You're doing a great job out there. Want to come over and rake a few in my yard?"

"Polly?" Claire says anxiously.

"Everything's fine," Polly says. There are burned eggs in a frying pan on the stove. Untouched coffee and toast on the table. Polly puts her arm around her mother, and she's surprised by how small Claire seems. "Really."

That night Charlie's fever breaks, but Amanda is still allowed to spend the night at Laurel's, and she's thrilled. Laurel makes up a bed for her on the wicker loveseat and they have homemade pizza and real lemonade for dinner. Laurel doesn't have a cassette player, so they sit in her car to hear Amanda's new tapes.

"This is how it would be if we were roommates," Amanda says. "Our boyfriends would have just left."

"They would have given us diamond necklaces," Laurel says.

"And pink and yellow roses," Amanda says.

"They'd give us white sports cars," Laurel adds. Her Datsun's battery is wearing down just from using the cassette player. "Porsches."

When they see the first star they both make a wish.

"Tell me what yours is," Laurel says.

"I can't," Amanda says. "It's too stupid."

"I won't laugh," Laurel says. "I promise."

"I wished I could have my braces off," Amanda says.

"That's not stupid," Laurel Smith tells her.

"It isn't?" Amanda says.

"It's a great wish," Laurel says. "Honest."

As they're walking back to the house the phone rings. It's Polly, for the third time, just checking on Amanda.

"She worries all the time," Amanda says when she gets off the phone.

"She probably just wanted to say good night," Laurel says.

Amanda goes into the bathroom and gets undressed. She's borrowing one of Laurel's nightgowns, and even though it's too big, it's beautiful; it's made out of soft pink flannel with a collar of lace. She's been given her own towel and washcloth and a little soap in the shape of a seashell. When she comes back into the living room, Amanda is so tired her eyes are closing. Laurel tucks her in beneath a cotton quilt.

"Wait till you hear the birds in the morning," Laurel says as she lowers the shades behind the couch. "They'll wake you up at dawn, so just go back to sleep."

"I'd rather get up and watch them," Amanda says.

"Then go to sleep now," Laurel tells her.

Laurel turns out the lights and starts for the bedroom, with the cat, Stella, dodging her steps.

"Laurel?" Amanda calls.

"Everything all right?" Laurel asks.

"Oh, yeah," Amanda says. "I was just wondering if you could leave a light on."

Laurel feels along the wall, then switches on the bright overhead light.

"Wait a minute," she says. She goes into the bedroom and

179

unplugs her lamp with the pink silk shade. Then she puts it behind the wicker couch and plugs it in.

"There," Laurel says, pleased by the rose-colored cast of light from the lamp.

"You'll talk to me, won't you?" Amanda asks.

Laurel sits down on the edge of the coffee table. "Do you want me to stay until you fall asleep?"

"No," Amanda says. "I mean afterward. When I'm dead."

"Honey, I can't do that," Laurel says evenly.

"Yes, you can." Amanda sits up and leans forward. "That's what you do. You're a medium."

"They were dreams," Laurel says. She takes one of Amanda's hands in her own. "That's all they were."

Amanda pulls her hand away and studies Laurel. "Maybe you could. You could if you really wanted to."

It's late now and there are night herons in the marsh, searching the shallow water.

"No," Laurel says. "Not even if I really want to."

"I thought you'd be able to talk to me," Amanda whispers.

Laurel swallows hard, then shakes her head no. Weak with disappointment, Amanda leans back, her head on the pillow.

"I'll dream about you," Laurel tells her.

"You will?" Amanda says.

"Always," Laurel says.

"You don't really have to stay with me until I fall asleep," Amanda says.

"That's okay," Laurel tells her. "I don't mind."

Amanda keeps her eyes closed, and after a while she hears Laurel get up. Laurel pulls the quilt over Amanda's shoulders, then goes into her bedroom and closes the door. But that's all right, Amanda knows she'll be able to sleep. She wishes she could stay here forever because she's not as afraid as she usually is at night. As she falls asleep, Amanda is absolutely certain she'll be the first one to wake up in the morning; she'll be the first to hear the birds call.

But Ed Reardon may be the first person awake in town; he's up long before dawn. He took Charlie's blood sample to the lab himself and told them to rush it so Polly wouldn't have to wait till Monday for an answer. They've promised to call in the test results by ten today. Ed Reardon knows he can't have fallen in love with Polly, but that's what it feels like. He's too raw; he's showing things he shouldn't. Mary wouldn't talk to him when she and the kids got back from her sister's, and Ed didn't even try to approach her. Now she comes downstairs in the dark and finds him in the kitchen, having a cup of instant coffee. Mary goes to the stove and puts up a kettle for real coffee.

"Is there something I should know about?" Mary says.

"It's a quarter to six," Ed says. "I don't want to fight."

Mary sits down across from him at the table. "Just tell me," she says.

She looks pretty with no makeup; she smells like sleep.

"Just tell me now and I won't ask you again," Mary says.

Ed knows that she means it. She doesn't hold a grudge, she forgives easily, and she's honest enough to expect other people to be equally honest. Ed knows that he's married to her. Whether or not he wants to be at this moment doesn't really matter.

"There's nothing you should know about," he tells her.

At a little after ten Ed calls Polly to let her know that Charlie's test results are negative.

"Thank God," Polly says. "I was going crazy. I was crazy."

"If his fever's broken and he's not coughing you can have Amanda come home," Ed says.

"How did you get the lab to run this on the weekend?" Polly asks him.

"I told them it was for you," Ed says.

181

They're both silent then. Charlie has the TV turned up and Claire is running the water in the sink. Mary and the kids are getting dressed so they can drive out to a farm and choose their pumpkin for Halloween.

"Well," Polly says finally, "I guess I'd better go."

"Me too," Ed Reardon says.

He listens to her hang up the phone, then he hangs up. He takes his jacket from the hall closet, then gets the car keys and goes outside.

"I don't believe this," Mary says when she comes outside and finds him in the car. "Get in," she tells the kids. "Are you actually coming with us?" she asks Ed.

He doesn't know whether he is or not until he turns the key in the ignition.

"Of course I am," Ed says. "Where else would I go?"

In Morrow, on Sunday, the market doesn't open till noon, and that's where Polly heads as soon as her parents leave to drive back to New York. Amanda will be back for dinner, and Polly wants everything to be special. God knows what Laurel Smith let her eat last night. God knows what they talked about.

Polly pulls in and parks, then gets a cart someone's left in the parking lot. She takes her shopping list out of her jacket pocket as she walks toward the market.

"It is you," Betsy Stafford says. "I wasn't sure from a distance."

Polly keeps walking, pushing her cart up the ramp to the sidewalk, headed toward the electronic swinging door.

"Polly, we have to talk," Betsy says.

You bitch, Polly thinks. She rolls her cart faster. The wheels squeak.

"I know you're mad," Betsy says.

Polly stops, frozen. If she had a gun she would turn and shoot

Betsy and think nothing of it. She would stay on to see the blood.

"I panicked," Betsy said. "I'm still panicking."

Polly turns then and looks at Betsy. Betsy's cart is filled with bags of groceries. Polly can see a sack of oranges, a gallon of chocolate-chip ice cream, rolls of paper towels.

"You would have done the same thing," Betsy says.

"I doubt it," Polly says. "I'm not that stupid or cruel."

"You think it doesn't kill me to keep the boys apart?"

"You're still breathing," Polly says.

"How do you think I feel when Sevrin won't talk to me? When he slams the door in my face? You think I like to hear my son crying at night?"

"Frankly, if you're worried about contamination I'm with Amanda more than Charlie is. Aren't you afraid I'll infect you? What if the scientists are wrong?" Polly knows she sounds hysterical, but she can't stop. "What if you use this shopping cart next time you're at the market? What if you pick up my germs?"

"This breaks my heart," Betsy whispers.

"No!" Polly tells her. "It makes you uncomfortable. It breaks my heart."

"Sevrin is all I have," Betsy says. "You have Charlie. Sevrin is my only child. I just couldn't take the risk." Betsy's face is crumpled; her eyes look swollen.

"Betsy, please," Polly says. She's exhausted and she doesn't want to think about any of this.

"I want you to understand!" Betsy says.

Polly closes her eyes and when she does she sees Charlie in bed with a fever of 102. She sees his head on the pillow and his pajama top open and damp with sweat. All this time when she thought she and Betsy were business partners she was wrong. Betsy was her friend.

183

"I do understand," Polly says. "Just don't ask me to forgive you. I don't know if Charlie and Sevrin ever will."

"I have a basementful of newts," Betsy says. She tries to laugh, but it sounds as if she's choking. "Some of the boys' specimens must have escaped and I think they're breeding down there."

"Your ice cream is melting," Polly says.

Betsy looks down at her cart and nods.

"I've got to pick up something for dinner," Polly says. "I want to make lamb chops for Amanda. I want to make baked potatoes and peas and chocolate pudding. Not that instant crap. The kind you have to stir."

"The instant can't be good for you," Betsy agrees. "It jells too fast."

Polly nods and walks away; she feels completely drained, powerless to do anything but cook meals no one wants, and to wait. But what is she waiting for? Nothing changes. Here is this man whom she loves beside her in bed and she can't touch him; here is her family, her house, the curtains she chose so carefully, the first photographs she was ever paid for taking, at Sevrin's birthday party. The only way Polly can fall asleep is to count backward from a thousand. She used to do this when she was a little girl; she used to twirl her hair with one finger while she counted, and in the morning she would wake up with knots on one side of her head.

Tonight she dreams that she has lost Amanda and cannot find her. She enters her dream through an alleyway made of stones. She can hear children crying, and the sound of shovels, methodically hitting against the earth. It's raining and the ground is slippery; as she runs, mud splashes up and coats her legs, turning them the color of blood.

This is what she knows: Someone has taken her daughter. Someone has put up a fence ringed with spikes. Someone is screaming in the distance. There are other children here, with no one to care for them, but Polly has no time for them. She runs faster. Her heart is pounding. She reaches the shelter she's looking for, and when she goes inside all she can see is one bed after another. Rows and rows of iron beds made up with white sheets. This is the children's house. This is the place where they're given food and water every day, but there is still no one to hold them. As she walks through the shelter, children cry out to her, babies lift their arms, begging to be picked up. They all look the same to her, that is what's horrible. They look like Amanda, but they're not. Polly knows she will recognize her own daughter; she must. There she is, in a small bed pushed up against a wall. Amanda can no longer speak, but Polly can tell she recognizes her. She wraps her in a sheet, and after they leave the shelter, after they step outside, the sheet trails in the mud and makes a hissing sound.

The alley she first entered by is the only way out, and, without seeing them, Polly knows there are guards. But all guards grow careless, they grow sleepy when their stomachs are full, when the screaming is in the distance and not right at their feet. So Polly crouches down low; it is dusk now, but that won't last forever. They will wait until dark. When no one is looking, when their backs are turned, Polly will hoist Amanda over her shoulder and make her way back to the alley. The only thing they really have to fear is a full moon, because in this dream even moonlight is dangerous.

185

14

THERE ARE SOME days when Amanda sleeps all day instead of going to school. There are days she's so nauseated she can't get off the bathroom floor. Her mother sits beside her on the tiles and runs a cool, wet washcloth along her forehead. They sit near the base of the toilet and her mother lifts her onto her lap and rocks back and forth and that makes her feel a little better. Things she used to love to eat she can't even look at anymore because her throat is all bunched up. Her father makes her a sweet mixture of spring water and honey and liquid protein, and on her bad days she sips from a plastic cup. The drink makes her think of bees and hot weather; it makes her think of cool pond water that looks green in the shallows.

On her good days she insists on going to school. Her parents have stopped trying to persuade her to stay home. Her mother packs a healthy lunch, which she never eats. Her father makes her take a vial of vitamins, which she always empties into a trash basket. On good days she goes to practice, and she always wears her leotard. She's so skinny she knows she looks awful, but she just couldn't stand to be in the gym without her leotard. She's been wearing her good-luck necklace to practice and, in spite of his strict rule about no jewelry, the coach never says a word about it to her, although last Tuesday he caught her sneaking a Life Saver and he treated her just like everyone else.

"Farrell," he called across the gym, and Amanda still doesn't know how he could possibly have spotted her from that distance. "Spit that out now!"

Today the coach has been really rough on the girls, and there's a wave of discontent on the bench. The next meet is against Clarkson, a school in a rich district; most of the girls on that team go to fancy gymnastics camps in the summer. The coach always goes crazy before a meet with Clarkson, and maybe that's why he's so hard on Jessie when she messes up her backflips.

"If you can't do it right, don't do it at all," the coach shouts. "Take it out of your routine."

Jessie walks back to the bench scowling and drenched with sweat. It's awful for anybody when the coach yells at her, but much worse for Jessie, since she has to go home with him. Amanda watches as Jessie sits down beside Evelyn Crowley. They've been spending a lot of time together, and now they put their heads close and whisper. Amanda knows what the problem is. Jessie's not tucking her legs in enough. Amanda could do a backflip in her sleep. She dreams about gymnastics moves, and in her dreams her body is strong, her legs don't ache.

Amanda waits until Evelyn Crowley goes to start her routine on the balance beam, then she goes over to where Jessie's sitting. Amanda has a slight limp now, but she doesn't think anyone can really notice. She sits down next to Jessie, but neither of them looks at the other.

"He's down on everybody today," Amanda says as she watches Evelyn mount the beam.

"He's a bastard," Jessie says. Anyone could tell how hard she's trying not to cry.

"He just wants you to be as good as you can be," Amanda says. The coach himself has told them this a million times.

"As good as you," Jessie says. She glares at Amanda. "That's what you mean."

"You forgot the 'was,' " Amanda says.

Jessie looks at her blankly.

"As good as I was," Amanda says.

They look away from each other and stare at the coach. He has a clipboard and a scoring sheet and he's rating every girl's performance.

"Coaches have to be mean," Amanda says. "That's their job."

"And obnoxious and fat and stupid," Jessie adds.

They both crack up over that.

"Evelyn's doing okay," Amanda says.

"Yeah," Jessie says grudgingly. "She's okay. She'll never be as good as you."

"Yeah," Amanda says. "Well, she might be."

As soon as they see the coach heading toward them they shut up, fast. The coach doesn't go for conversations on the bench.

"What the hell is this?" Jack Eagan says when he reaches them. "Get off your butt," he tells Jessie. "You're not leaving here until I see a perfect backflip."

Jessie shoots him a murderous look, then gets off the bench to practice.

"She needs to tuck her legs in," Jack Eagan says. He sits down next to Amanda, the clipboard between them. "Think we have a chance against Clarkson?"

Amanda starts to shrug, but when she looks at him she realizes he's serious. He wants her opinion.

"Evelyn's got a real good chance at scoring."

189

The coach nods, so Amanda goes on.

"Sue Sherman could rate really high on her vaulting."

"You could be right," Jack Eagan says. "Do me a favor."

Amanda nods, speechless.

"If you're going to wear that necklace to the Clarkson meet, wear it inside your leotard. I don't want a mutiny just because one girl is wearing jewelry. Okay?"

"Okay," Amanda says. She had no idea she'd be allowed to go to an away meet with them; she hasn't really been certain that she's still on the team anymore.

"If you get a chance you might want to mention tucking her legs in to Jessie," the coach says. "She sure doesn't listen to me."

"If you want me to I will," Amanda says.

"Atta girl," Jack Eagan says. "I knew I could depend on you."

Polly is waiting for Amanda after practice, parked in the semicircular driveway reserved for buses right in front of the school. It kills Polly to see how slowly Amanda is walking, but she stays where she is instead of jumping out to help; she lets the motor idle. She can no longer tell the difference between her anger and her sorrow. Her house might as well say CONTAMINATED on the front door. When she walks into a shop, even when she goes to the gas station to fill up the Blazer, people ignore her, people she's known for years, neighbors she used to have coffee with, shop owners who know her by name. If Amanda had cancer or a brain tumor, they'd be bringing her casseroles and cakes. They'd be filling up her gas tank for free.

Polly hates her neighbors, but it's herself she blames. She's guilty even in her dreams. Last night she dreamed there was a deserted silver trailer on the edge of town. Everyone in town knew about the trailer; they tried to stop Polly from going inside, but she opened the metal door. Inside there were piles of filth, the kitchen cupboards held no food, there was no running water, a dozen white cats darted beneath the furniture.

The woman who lived in the trailer tried to hide herself once the door had been opened. She was skin and bones, along her arms were welts the color of violets. The whole town knew about her; it was they who kept her there. Shut the door, they called to Polly. Shut it fast.

Polly stood in the doorway and cursed everyone in town; frogs came out of her mouth, and her words turned into wasps. She vowed she would find this woman a decent place to live, even if no one else cared. She would get her food and water, heat, a bed with clean sheets. The woman crawled out from her hiding place; her face was wet with tears. In gratitude she reached up for Polly and kissed the back of Polly's hand. In her dream, Polly grew cold because she knew what no one else in town knew. She knew that the minute everyone's back was turned, she would find some running water, the hotter the better, and wash away that kiss.

When she woke from her dream, Polly was sick to her stomach. She still despises herself for her own dream, she feels tainted by her own night fears. It's as if the idea of a plague can unlock a terrible, deep panic that no one can stop, not with hard facts or with dreams. More than ever, Polly is convinced that she did not protect her baby, she could not stop this from happening to her little girl.

Amanda is beaming when she gets into the Blazer. Jessie actually listened when Amanda suggested she tuck her legs in tighter for her backflips. Amanda can't stop thinking about the coach asking for her help. She feels very grown-up, like an assistant coach or something.

"You've got to talk to Dad," Amanda tells Polly as soon as she gets into the car. "I have to go to the Clarkson meet. The coach is depending on me."

"I'll discuss it with him," Polly says, knowing Ivan won't like the idea.

"Don't discuss it," Amanda says. "Tell him he has to let me go."

"I'll talk to him," Polly says.

Today at lunch Polly met Laurel Smith at the South Street Café, across the street from the gift shop. Laurel wore a plaid skirt and a bulky gray sweater and her hair was twisted into French braids. Polly was struck by how young she looked. Polly has begun to wonder if women without children don't age as quickly; they've had all those extra years of sleeping through the night.

Polly ordered a spinach salad and coffee, Laurel a hamburger, fries, and a vanilla milkshake. It was less like eating lunch with a friend than taking one of her daughter's pals out for a treat. After they'd eaten, Laurel pushed her plate away, then leaned toward Polly, her elbows on the table.

"Amanda has a wish," Laurel said.

Polly put her coffee cup down. She didn't want to hear about wishes; one more thing Amanda wouldn't be able to have.

"She wants her braces off," Laurel Smith said.

They stared at each other and then they both burst out laughing.

"Not Bruce Springsteen over for dinner?" Polly managed to say. She knew from the pitch of her laughter that she was getting hysterical. "Not a trip to Hawaii or Disney World?"

Polly gasped for breath. Laurel handed her a glass of water and she gulped some down.

"Oh, God," Polly said. "It's such a little wish."

And now, driving home with Amanda, Polly tries to think what her last wish would have been when she was eleven going on twelve. She would have wanted to be taken out to a nightclub, to be allowed to stay up till midnight and drink pink champagne with cherries floating in the glass. Given the choice of anyone, she would have wanted her father to be her date for the evening. He would have worn a tuxedo, the kind with tails, she would have worn a pair of blue silk high heels.

"I just hope the meet isn't on the same day as the orthodontist," Polly says at a stop sign on Ash Street. She looks over at Amanda, who's staring at her. "You didn't think you were going to wear your braces forever, did you?"

Amanda leans over and throws her arms around Polly. "You're the greatest mother in the world," she crows.

Polly laughs and untangles herself from Amanda. "I'm driving!" Polly says, but she reaches for Amanda's hand and squeezes it.

"It can't be on the same day as the meet," Amanda says. She thinks it over. "It has to be before."

"Dr. Crosbie may be busy," Polly says. "Did you ever think of that?"

"He just has to take some pliers and pull them off," Amanda says. "Maybe he can do it today."

Polly grins and tells Amanda she's certain the orthodontist is booked for this afternoon, but as soon as they get home she phones Crosbie's office. She's shocked to discover his appointments are filled, not just for today but for the next three weeks.

"We can't wait three weeks!" Polly tells his secretary. "My daughter is dying! She can't wait three weeks."

Crosbie's secretary puts Polly on hold, and while she's listening to the taped Muzak, which is automatically switched on, Polly opens the refrigerator so she can think about supper instead of Amanda. There's enough lettuce and cucumbers for a salad. There's a small steak she'd like Amanda to have, but it's not enough for all of them and she doesn't want Amanda to feel uncomfortable about being singled out for a special meal. Polly decides she'll just make her quick meatloaf. She's mixing breadcrumbs and

Parmesan cheese into the chopped meat when the secretary finally takes her off hold to tell her there are no appointments. Polly rips a paper towel off the roll above the sink and wipes off her hands.

"He must have an appointment free for her," she tells the secretary.

"I just want to make certain. This is Amanda Farrell we're talking about, right? Dr. Crosbie can't see her," the secretary says firmly.

"He has to make time for her," Polly says.

"Dr. Crosbie isn't seeing patients with AIDS," the secretary says.

Polly hangs up the phone and sits down. Of course, she thinks. She can even understand it. She just can't believe it. There are still some breadcrumbs on her hands. She can hear Charlie down in the basement, and she wonders if he's spending so much time alone not out of choice, because he's lost Sevrin, but because the kids at school don't want any more to do with him than Dr. Crosbie wants with Amanda. Polly goes downstairs, taking the steps two at a time. Charlie has all four hamsters in one cage while he cleans out the other two cages. His field mice are in an old bird cage and he's already fed them and filled up their water bottle. Polly goes over to him and grabs him. Charlie faces her, frightened.

"Are the kids saying anything to you?" Polly asks.

"What kids?" Charlie says.

"The kids at school!" Polly says. "Are they not friends with you because of Amanda?"

"I'm not friends with them," Charlie corrects her. Then he adds, "Your fingernails are hurting me."

Polly drops his arm.

"They wouldn't play with me before we had the assembly,

but they're okay now," Charlie says. "Not that I care. I mean, I need them if I want to play soccer, but that's all."

Polly sits down on a wooden stool. Charlie watches her, sweating. Most of what he's told her is the truth, but he'd say anything to get her out of the basement. The Minolta is on the shelf by the hamster food. Next to the camera are two rolls of undeveloped film and a light meter he stole from the darkroom, which he's been hoping to use the next time he goes to the pond.

"People are stupid," Polly says.

"Yeah," Charlie quickly agrees. If she turns her back for a minute, he thinks he may be able to throw a plastic garbage bag over the camera.

"They're frightened when they shouldn't be and they're not frightened when there's really something to be scared of."

"I know," Charlie nods.

That's when Polly sees the Minolta.

"People are definitely weird," Charlie says.

If this were July or even the beginning of August, Polly would have his head for fooling around with the Minolta. She'd ask him why in hell he didn't ask her first. Why he thought she'd ever let him use it when there's an old Polaroid she might consider lending him. But it's October, and it's cold down here in the basement, and she doesn't care about her camera. Although, clearly, somebody does. The Minolta is in its case and the rolls of film are in a neat line.

"Do you ever see Barry Wagoner? Isn't he in your class?" Polly asks.

"Barry's a jerk," Charlie tells her. "I've got to finish these cages, Mom. I've got two males in together and they might beat each other up if I don't move them soon."

Polly nods and goes upstairs. She can hear the cassette player in Amanda's room whirling backward, rewinding a tape. She

195

can hear the clang of metal as Charlie empties out old cedar chips from a cage into a trash barrel. Polly gets out the Yellow Pages and riffles through until she finds DENTISTS. She calls the three orthodontists she finds listed on the North Shore, but not one will agree to see a patient who isn't his own. Polly puts the Yellow Pages away after that.

These days it's dark by five-thirty; Polly watches the light fade and she's still sitting in the kitchen when Ivan gets home from the institute. As soon as she sees him, Polly begins to sob. Ivan sits down across from her at the table and watches her cry.

"Are you all right?" he says when Polly stops sobbing.

Polly nods and tells Ivan that the one wish Amanda has will never be granted; no orthodontist will touch her.

"Oh, yes they will," Ivan says darkly.

He gets up and goes to the phone.

"Crosbie won't do it," Polly tells him.

"Fuck Crosbie," Ivan says. He dials Brian's number. He has to wait for Adelle to carry the phone into Brian's bedroom. He tells Brian exactly what they need, an orthodontist who's willing to work on an AIDS patient, and Brian tells him he'll have to call around and get back to him. When he hangs up the phone, Ivan realizes that Polly's been studying him.

"The friend you bought flowers for," Polly says.

Ivan goes to the refrigerator and gets himself a beer. "Let's not cook tonight," he says. He feels a sharp pain all along his spine. "Let's get pizza."

"He's the one who's dying," Polly says.

"That's right," Ivan says savagely. "The one who's twenty-eight years old."

Polly nods to his beer. "Can I have one of those?"

Ivan brings another beer to the table.

"Is your friend a dentist or something?" Polly asks.

Ivan laughs in spite of himself. "He worked on an AIDS hot-line. He has friends."

"Oh," Polly says. She thinks it over. "Good."

Ivan is out picking up the pizza and Amanda is setting the table when the phone rings.

"It's Brian," the voice on the other end of the line says.

"Brian," Polly says. "Oh, Brian." She can't believe how young he sounds, how far away. "Ivan's out, he's getting a pizza."

"That's okay," Brian says. "You're Amanda's mother, I can give you the secret password. It's Rothstein."

"Oh, God," Polly says. "The orthodontist."

"Bernard Rothstein," Brian says. "He'll do it."

Polly is waiting out on the porch when Ivan gets back. They stand with the pizza between them; heat rises from the cardboard box.

"He called," Polly tells Ivan. Ivan reaches and touches her face; her cheek is cold and soft. "He found someone," Polly says.

"That's good," Ivan says. "That's real good. I was a madman. I was ready to kill some poor innocent dentist."

Polly can't help but laugh. "Stop it," she says.

"I mean it. Some poor unsuspecting jerk would be filling a cavity and in I'd walk with a shotgun."

Polly is laughing so hard he can't understand what she's saying.

"What?" Ivan says, mystified.

"You don't have a gun," Polly manages to say.

"A bow and arrow," Ivan says. "A fly rod."

The back door opens and Charlie leans his head out. "Mom?" he says, puzzled when he hears Polly laughing.

"Who were you expecting?" Polly says. "Count Dracula?"

"Is that Mom?" Amanda says.

Amanda has come up behind Charlie and she peers past him, out to the porch. Polly spins around in a silly dance; the children can just about make her out in the dark. Ivan laughs low down in his throat; he sounds the way he used to.

"They're crazy," Amanda whispers to her brother.

"Yep," Charlie says. "They sure are."

The day before Amanda's appointment with Dr. Rothstein, Polly phones Ed Reardon to let him know that they won't be home at the time he usually comes over. Ed has gotten into the habit of stopping by the house on his way home for dinner. Sometimes he and Polly have a beer together; they sit at the kitchen table and talk about perfect vacations. Polly's first choice is France; Ed always argues the merits of a month in Edgartown. Neither of them will get to half the places they've talked about, not alone, not together. Ed isn't fooling himself; he knows theirs are less the conversations of lovers than of two people at a wake. And besides, he's a man who fulfills his obligations, even though lately he feels like a charlatan. He's supposed to be able to cure his patients and he can't, and yet for no reason at all people continue to believe in him. Tonight he is a special guest, a witness really, at a school board hearing. It's the school district's policy to hold such a hearing should a petition surface like the one asking for Linda Gleason's resignation. Two more children have been pulled out of Cheshire, but other than that the furor is dying down a bit, or maybe it's simply gone underground. Some of the teachers who signed the petition against Linda Gleason have gone out of their way to be friendly to her; maybe they're embarrassed, or maybe they're just afraid for their jobs. After the hearing, Ed and Linda Gleason walk out to their cars together. It's a damp night, and the air smells like wood-smoke.

"Thanks for supporting me," Linda says. "Little do they know I'm thinking of quitting."

"Me too," Ed says.

They both take out their car keys.

"Not that we will," Linda Gleason adds.

At home they both have children waiting, suppers in the oven, still warm.

"We could get in our cars and drive to New Mexico," Ed says. "It would take them years to find us."

Linda looks at him carefully. It's hard to tell whether or not he's kidding.

"Forget about all this for a night," Linda advises him. "Take two aspirins and call me in the morning."

"I'd still feel the same way," Ed says.

Of course, he doesn't mention wanting Polly beside him in that car headed to New Mexico. Ed knows that to say it out loud would make him seem like a desperate man. He goes on with his life, with his responsibilities, as best he can. He goes home, he gets into bed beside his wife, but he doesn't feel that he's where he's supposed to be until the morning, when he drives to the Farrells'. Ivan has been making pancakes; he's still wearing an apron.

"A day off," Ivan says as he lets Ed inside.

"For some of us," Ed jokes, but he's shocked seeing them all together for breakfast. He has been thinking of them in pieces instead of as a family. Polly waves from the counter. She's pouring boiling water through the coffee filter; she's wearing a linen suit and high heels. Ed can't remember ever having seen her so dressed up before. He feels dazed. Something inside him rattles as Charlie and Amanda argue over who gets the syrup first.

"Just in time for breakfast," Polly tells Ed.

Ed stands behind Amanda and gently puts his hand on the

199

base of her neck. He squeezes slightly, as a greeting, but also to feel her swollen glands. Amanda has taken two bites of her pancake, that's all.

"No time for me," Ed says. "I have approximately three hundred office visits today."

He's going to get into his car and drive to his office. He's going to see patients all morning, then order a sandwich from the South Street Café and have it at his desk. At a little after six, he'll drive home. He knows what he's going to do and when he has to do it, and none of it includes running off. Not to New Mexico, or Martha's Vineyard, or France.

"Save your first smile without braces for me," Ed tells Amanda.

"Not a chance," Ivan says. "I've already got dibs on that."

"Good luck," Ed says to Amanda, but he's looking at Polly.

"Thanks for stopping by," Polly calls, as if it had been a social visit; she makes certain not to turn around until he's gone.

They drop Charlie off at school, then drive south on I-93, toward Boston. At the office in Brookline, Dr. Rothstein takes longer removing the braces than they'd expected. Polly and Ivan hold hands in the waiting room. They're trying not to think about the bill he'll send them or what their insurance will and will not cover for the rest of Amanda's medical treatments. They'll sell the Blazer if they have to. Polly can always go back to photographing weddings and birthday parties. She'd be better at that now, she wouldn't feel so compromised.

Up until the very last minute, when Dr. Rothstein actually came into the waiting room to welcome them, Polly and Ivan weren't certain he wouldn't change his mind. When he came out of his office he shook Amanda's hand, then led her along the hallway. Once she was in the chair, he put on two pairs of rubber gloves and a surgical mask and he got to work. He talks to Amanda mostly about his dogs; he's a fanatic about West

Highland terriers. He shows them all over New England, and he's about to breed them, in case Amanda knows anyone who's looking for a puppy with great bloodlines. Amanda's mouth hurts from keeping it open for so long, but she's used to that from visits to Dr. Crosbie. She grunts sometimes when Dr. Rothstein leaves places in his conversation for a comment. He used to have collies, but he couldn't take all their shedding. He can fit both his Westies into a shopping bag and sneak them onto airplanes and trains. They're so well behaved they never make a sound.

When he uses the drill to cut through the metal wires, Amanda closes her eyes. The noise goes right through her and she holds onto the arms of her chair because the braces hurt just as much coming off as they did going on. Dr. Rothstein is wearing protective goggles over his eyes; he doesn't mention the fact that she's sick, but he's very nice to her. Never paper-train a dog, he tells her, if you do you'll just have one more habit to break him of. Amanda nods, agreeing with him. He puts something metal into a metal bowl and the sound sends shivers down Amanda's spine.

"Think about a Westie puppy," Dr. Rothstein says. "I'd give you pick of the litter."

When he's done, Amanda rinses out her mouth and spits into the little sink. She runs her tongue over her teeth. The naked enamel feels cold. Dr. Rothstein takes off his goggles, his mask, and his gloves. After he scrubs up he takes a mirror and faces Amanda.

"Ready?" he asks her.

Amanda nods, although she's not sure she is. What if she's uglier than she was before? What if her teeth are just as crooked?

"You're sure?" the orthodontist asks.

"I'm sure," Amanda says.

He holds up the mirror and Amanda takes a deep breath,

which she doesn't let out till she sees her face looming in front of her. She leans forward and tentatively opens her mouth. Then she smiles. And even though she tries to keep her mouth closed, she's still smiling when she walks out into the waiting room because now she knows. She would have been beautiful.

15

No one comes to their door on Halloween night. They can hear whoops of laughter as children outside go careening down the sidewalks, ringing doorbells and rattling their bags of candy. In the front hallway there's a bowl of Milky Ways and Almond Joys and a glass jar of pennies for UNICEF. Charlie, who advised everyone he was too old for trick-or-treating, has the TV turned on. At a little after eight, Ivan sits down beside him on the couch and tosses him a Milky Way. They might as well eat them, no one else will.

"What are we watching?" Ivan says as he unwraps a candy bar for himself. Amanda and Polly are upstairs in Amanda's room playing Scrabble in bed; Amanda has a sore throat, and every so often Polly comes downstairs for cough drops or tea.

"*Halloween III,*" Charlie says flatly.

There's someone with a big knife and a lot of terrified teenage girls.

"I don't think you're old enough for this," Ivan says.

"I've already seen it," Charlie tells him. "It gets really gross."

"What do you say we go trick-or-treating together?" Ivan suggests.

"Dad," Charlie says tiredly. "I really don't want to. Really."

When the doorbell rings, Charlie and Ivan look at each other.

"Trick-or-treaters," Ivan says triumphantly.

He grabs a couple of candy bars and goes to the door. There's a grown-up witch out there, in a black cape and tall black hat. Ivan stares at her and holds fast to the Milky Ways.

"It's all right," Laurel Smith tells him. "I'm a good witch."

Ivan laughs and opens the door. When Laurel comes inside there's a rush of cold, sweet air. There are some yellow leaves stuck to the bottom of her black boots. Over each eyelid Laurel wears a streak of silver shadow.

"It's a witch," Ivan calls to Charlie. "What's this?" he says to Laurel when he notices the wicker basket on her arm.

"Treats," Laurel says.

"You're a little confused," Ivan says. "We're supposed to give you something."

Charlie stands in the living room doorway, his mouth open. His feet are bare and his shirt is small for him; a line of skin shows along his stomach and his wrists look too narrow. Laurel Smith reaches into her wicker basket and pulls out a paper bag marked with his name; inside there are chocolates and a yo-yo that glows in the dark.

"This is for you," Laurel Smith says.

"That's okay," Charlie says. He hasn't moved from the doorway. "I don't need anything."

Ivan takes the paper bag. "I'll save it for him," he tells Laurel. "In case he changes his mind."

Charlie backs up, so that Laurel Smith can get past him and go up the stairs. Even dressed all in black, she's really pretty. Charlie wants whatever she's brought him, but he wanted to go trick-or-treating, too. He and Sevrin had both planned to steal shaving cream from their fathers and attack every parked car on the street. Charlie goes back into the living room and throws himself on the couch; he turns up the volume on the TV until he can no longer hear Laurel's footsteps upstairs in the hallway.

Laurel knocks, twice, then opens the bedroom door. She's already talked this surprise visit over with Polly, but Polly acts just as surprised as Amanda when Laurel swirls into the room.

"Trick or treat!" Laurel grins.

"Oh, my goodness, a witch!" Polly shouts.

Amanda gets out from under the covers and jumps up so quickly that the Scrabble board tilts and letters fall all over the floor.

"You're so beautiful!" Amanda says in a hoarse, whispery voice.

"Well, thank you!" Laurel says. "And just for that, I've got a basketful of treats for you."

Polly gets up. "I'll make some tea," she tells them. "Don't eat everything before I get back."

Laurel sits down next to Amanda on the bed, the wicker basket on her lap. Amanda's nightgown is too big for her and her hair is knotted. She moves closer to Laurel.

"Are there a lot of kids out trick-or-treating?" Amanda asks.

Laurel Smith nods.

"I'm afraid," Amanda says.

"I know," Laurel says.

Laurel leans down and puts her wicker basket on the floor. Inside there are chocolate tarts, and strands of plastic beads that look like rubies and pearls. There are chocolates made in Holland in the shape of apples and oranges and a gold headband with rhinestone chips. Tonight, as Laurel drove along the marsh road, there was a big full moon, so perfect and white it was like a child's drawing of a moon.

205

"I'm really afraid," Amanda whispers in a small, raw voice.

As Laurel Smith puts her arms around the girl, her black cape makes a rustling sound. They hold fast to each other, rocking, and they stay that way for a long time, not because they think it will change anything, but because they don't want to let go of each other just yet.

Amanda's temperature doesn't begin to rise until midnight. Once it begins, her fever keeps on climbing until the following afternoon, the day of the Clarkson meet, when it reaches 103. Amanda has awful pains in her joints, especially in her wrists and her knees. When she breathes it hurts, when she tries to turn over she cries. She's miserable and upset about missing the meet, and she refuses to eat or drink. Polly, who's afraid of dehydration, brings up glasses of water and lemonade.

"You have to drink," Polly tells Amanda, but Amanda insists she can't swallow.

All that night Ivan and Polly take turns sitting up with Amanda, forcing her to take small sips of water, carrying her to the bathroom whenever she has to go because her legs hurt too much to walk. Outside, it begins to rain, a cold rain that rattles the windows and shakes the last few leaves from the trees. At five-thirty in the morning Polly phones Ed Reardon and tells his wife that she needs Ed immediately. He's at their house before six. He manages to talk Amanda into swallowing some water, and, as soon as he listens to her lungs, he knows it won't be long until he has to check her back into Children's. Polly has not mentioned anything to him about difficulty in breathing, but Amanda's lungs are filled with fluid.

"You're having trouble breathing," Ed says.

"No, I'm not," Amanda says stubbornly.

"Okay," Ed says to her. He knows she is inches from another

case of pneumocystis. It's this kind of recurrence he's been afraid of all along.

"Try to sleep," he tells Amanda.

"Can you send Charlie up?" Amanda asks. "Just for a minute."

"Sure thing," Ed Reardon says.

He goes downstairs to the kitchen, where Polly and Ivan are waiting. Charlie is at the table eating an English muffin with peanut butter. He's still in his pajamas and he looks sleepy.

"She wants to see you for a minute, Charlie old man," Ed tells him.

"Me?" Charlie says, surprised and a little frightened.

"Go on," Ed Reardon tells him.

Charlie looks at his father, who nods at him. As soon as Charlie's out of the room Ed says, "Get someone to stay with Charlie. She may have to go back into the hospital tomorrow. Maybe even tonight."

"No," Polly says. "Not this time."

As long as Amanda is home she's just a sick girl, down with the flu, like hundreds, thousands of other sick girls.

"We all knew this might happen," Ed Reardon says.

Ivan turns to the wall and punches it. Bits of plaster fall onto the floor like white dust. Ivan is crying; he's not making a sound, but he's shaking all over. It's a terrible thing to see; his fury paralyzes Polly. Ed goes over to Ivan and puts a hand on his shoulder, but Ivan jerks away. When Ivan finally does turn toward Ed his face is wet.

"This is my daughter!" Ivan says. "She's eleven years old."

Upstairs, Charlie stands at the threshold of Amanda's room. He knocks once on the open door.

"Come here," Amanda says when she sees him. "Hurry."

Charlie swallows and walks inside.

"I want you to see the coach. You have to tell him why I wasn't at the meet yesterday."

Amanda's voice is hot and hoarse. She sounds upset, crazy even.

"Okay," Charlie says.

"You have to explain," Amanda says.

"All right. I will."

"You won't forget?" Amanda says.

Charlie shakes his head. She looks old lying there in bed. She looks too white.

"Will you find out what the score was for me?" Amanda asks.

"I'll come home right after school," Charlie tells her.

Charlie feels scared all the way to school. He bikes hard and he's sweating when he gets to his classroom. He watches the clock all morning. They're still on the Civil War, but Charlie couldn't listen even if he wanted to. At eleven they all get lined up to go to the art room. They have art every Friday, and Charlie has been working on a papier-mâché brontosaurus whose head keeps falling off. Charlie waits to make certain he'll be at the end of the line. In the hallway, he lags behind the other kids, and when they start to file into the art room, he ducks into the boys' room. He stays in a closed stall, his heart pounding, until he hears it grow quiet in the hall. Then he goes back out and heads for the gym. He passes a fifth-grade teacher, but Charlie just acts as if he has a right to be in the hall, and the teacher doesn't bother to ask where he's going.

When he gets to the gym, Charlie feels even more scared. He's been feeling like this all day, and he can't shake it. There's a class in the gym, but Charlie opens the door anyway and slips inside. The fifth-graders are here for their gym period, and Charlie recognizes some of the boys who are always giving the third- and fourth-graders a hard time. Some boys are practicing on the rings, and lines of girls and boys are taking turns tumbling.

Charlie doesn't see Coach Eagan because he's way in the back, holding the tail end of the rope as a boy shimmies up toward the ceiling.

"Hey, you!" the coach yells from across the gym.

Charlie turns to him, rigid.

"That's right, you! Are you supposed to be here?"

Some of the fifth-graders snicker.

"Well, go on," the coach says to Charlie. "Out."

Charlie stands where he is.

The coach hands the rope over to a tall boy, then walks toward Charlie.

"Listen, son," the coach says. "This is no joke. Get to where you're supposed to be now."

"Amanda sent me to talk to you," Charlie says. He wishes now he had peed when he was in the boys' room.

The coach looks at Charlie carefully. He doesn't know many of the kids from the lower grades; Rose usually teaches their gym periods.

"I'm her brother, Charlie." Charlie's voice breaks. "She couldn't come to the meet because she was sick. She just wanted you to know that."

The coach nods and stands next to Charlie. He puts one hand on Charlie's head. His hand is heavy. Charlie could swear it weighs ten pounds.

"She's a great kid," Jack Eagan says.

"Yes, sir," Charlie quickly agrees. He doesn't know if he's ever actually called anyone sir before. He looks straight ahead, afraid to move. Directly across from him, a boy fumbles on the rings.

"That was my best event," Jack Eagan says when he notices Charlie staring at the rings. He takes his hand off Charlie's head. "Ever try it?"

"No, sir," Charlie says.

"Come on," the coach says. When Charlie doesn't follow him, he turns back and says, "Come on," again, as if Charlie were deaf. When they get to the rings the coach says, "Get off, Simpson."

The boy having trouble drops to his feet.

"Let's see you get up," the coach says to Charlie.

Charlie looks at the coach. Then, terrified, he leaps as high as he can and grabs onto the rings.

"Good," the coach says. "Now pull yourself up."

Charlie can feel every muscle in his body as he pulls himself up.

"Stick your legs straight out," the coach says.

Charlie does it, even though his legs are shaking. It's crazy, but he could swear he feels himself growing stronger. His legs stop shaking and then he lets go and falls to his feet.

"Not bad," the coach says. "Ever think about gymnastics?"

"No, sir. I hate sports. Except for soccer."

Jack Eagan nods, displeased. As far as he's concerned, soccer isn't even an American sport.

"What grade are you in?"

"Third," Charlie says.

"Well, let me know if you change your mind by fifth," the coach says.

"All right," Charlie says.

The coach gets his clipboard and writes Charlie a note.

"Just give this to your teacher if she asks where you've been."

"Amanda wanted to know what the score was last night," Charlie says.

"Tell her we won," Jack Eagan says.

Charlie gets home at a little after two. His father is home and his grandparents are already there, even though it's only

Friday. Charlie knows things are bad because it's so quiet in the house, and when he tries to go upstairs, his father stops him.

"We don't want any noise up there," Ivan tells him.

"I have to tell her something," Charlie says.

"It can wait," Ivan says.

"No, it can't!" Charlie insists.

Charlie starts to run up the stairs, and when his father follows him and yanks him by his arm, Charlie pulls free and hits Ivan. He hits him hard, and then, terrified by what he's done, Charlie backs away. His breathing is raspy and his chest hurts. "Sorry," he says. Charlie can't look at his father, but he can hear Ivan breathing hard, too.

Ivan sits down on the stairs. He looks tired and he looks old and that just makes Charlie feel worse.

"What do you have to tell her that's so important?" Ivan says.

"She asked me to find out if her team won," Charlie says. "Last night."

"Well?" Ivan says.

"Well, they did," Charlie says. His face is hot and he feels as if he's going to cry. "That's all."

"I'll tell her," Ivan says. "Do your homework downstairs today."

"Why?" Charlie says, nervous.

"Because I said to," Ivan tells him. He gets up and starts to go upstairs, then he thinks better of it. He goes back down to the bottom of the stairs. "Because Amanda is very sick," he says.

"Sick enough to die?" Charlie says.

"Yes," Ivan says. "Sick enough to die."

Ivan stands there on the stairs, crying.

"Okay," Charlie says, after a while. "I'll do my homework downstairs."

211

Ivan wipes his eyes and nods. "Good boy," he says.

Upstairs, Polly and Claire are trying to keep Amanda's fever down. Amanda has strictly forbidden her father's and grandfather's presence in the room when she's undressed, and as soon as she sees Ivan she tries to grab the sheet to hide herself.

"Charlie has a message for you," Ivan tells Amanda. "You won last night."

Amanda smiles and holds the sheet tighter.

"Out of here," Claire tells Ivan. "No men allowed. Isn't that right?" she says to Amanda.

Amanda nods and Ivan backs out of the room.

"This always helps," Claire says. She soaks a washcloth in a basin of water, then runs the cloth along Amanda's bare arms.

"Ooh," Amanda says, and she shivers.

Claire and Polly look at each other across the bed. Claire didn't have time to pack the way she usually does, and she's borrowed a dress from Polly that pulls across the front where it buttons. As soon as they're done sponging her down, Polly and Claire quickly pull the covers up over Amanda. Polly is fine until she thinks of a time, long ago, when she had a fever and her mother sponged her down all afternoon; she never once left the room, except to get more cool water.

"Go lie down for a few minutes," Claire tells Polly. Polly nods and goes to her room, but she doesn't lie down. When Ivan comes looking, she's still sitting on the edge of the bed. Ivan sits down next to her and runs his hand down her back. Polly looks at him as if she didn't know him.

"Come downstairs," Ivan says. "Your mother's made coffee. You know your father always says she makes the best coffee in the world."

Polly shakes her head; then she gets up and goes to the closet. She rummages on the shelves, behind the shoes, until she finds

what she's looking for. Her old Polaroid. There are two boxes
of film cartridges beside it.

"Polly," Ivan says.

She ignores him. She flips open the flash.

"The last good picture I took of her was before the summer.
I don't have time to develop film, so this way I'll have the photograph right now. What if it was happening and I didn't have a
picture of her?"

"It is happening," Ivan says.

"I haven't taken one picture of her with her braces off, but
you don't give a damn," Polly says. "Nobody gives a damn."
She rips open the box of film and slides it into the Polaroid.
"Stop looking at me," Polly says to Ivan when she's loaded the
camera. "I'm not insane."

Ivan tries to laugh, but his voice cracks. He gets up and starts
to walk to Polly.

"Stop where you are!" Polly says.

Ivan stands in the center of their room. His hands reach down
as though gravity were claiming him. He's wearing a blue shirt,
a pair of brown corduroy pants, an old sweater that has leather
patches on the elbows. Polly lifts the camera and takes his photograph. There is a flash of light, then a wrenching sound as the
Polaroid spits out the photograph.

"There you are," Polly says.

She walks to Ivan and hands him the photograph. As his photograph develops, from a blank white space to his image, Polly
holds Ivan tightly. He smells good, and he feels good, too, the
way he always has; this could be years ago, this could be the
first day they met. She has never told anyone, but she knew as
soon as she saw him that she'd marry Ivan. It was less love at
first sight than some deep knowledge that he was the man she
would someday fall in love with.

213

Polly goes out into the hall with her camera. She stops outside Amanda's room and looks in. Al is sitting on a chair by the bed. He'd been reading the comics to Amanda, but she's fallen asleep and the *Globe* is open on his lap.

"Hi, kid," he says softly to Polly when he sees her.

Amanda's hair is fanned out on the pillow. She's curled up, knees to chest, and her breathing is thick and loud. When Polly leaves this room she will phone Ed Reardon and ask him to meet them at the hospital. But right now she lifts the Polaroid and takes her daughter's photograph. The night Amanda was born there was lightning. Polly could feel the air pressure pushing down inside her body, and the first thing she thought when her water broke was, "Oh, no. I don't want to lose this baby," because that's what it felt like. Giving birth, no longer having her child within her seemed like a terrible loss. And when they held Amanda up and Polly saw her for the first time, she burst into tears. All these years later she can still remember what that moment felt like, she can still remember the lightning in the sky.

Polly stands beside her father, her hand on his shoulder, until Amanda opens her eyes.

"Hi," Amanda says when she sees them watching her.

"We're going to the hospital," Polly says.

Amanda nods and sits up a bit. "I just want to do one thing," she says. "I want to make out a will."

"Absolutely not," Polly says quickly. "That's ridiculous."

Amanda looks at her grandfather, and she's relieved when he nods.

"Dad!" Polly says when he gets up and goes to Amanda's desk.

Al gets a notebook and a Bic pen. He comes back to Polly and puts his arm around her.

"Let her do this," Al says, softly, so Amanda will not hear.

Polly bites her lip and nods. She has to turn away when Al sits down and opens the notebook, but she doesn't leave the room.

"I want Jessie to have all my jewelry," Amanda says. "Most of it's in my jewelry box, but I have some hidden in my top drawer. I want you and Grandma to have my art folder."

"Ah," Al says. "An art folder." All he has to do is write down the words and not think about them.

"I want Laurel to have all my cassettes and my cassette player."

"Laurie?" Al asks. He knows how important it is for him to get this right.

"Laurel," Amanda corrects him. "I don't have too much that Charlie would want, but he can have my gym bag, for collecting specimens. I want my mom and dad to have everything else."

"I've got that all down," Al says. He finishes writing and puts down the pen.

"I think I have to sign my name to it," Amanda says.

"You're right," Al says. He brings the notebook over to the bed and puts the pen in Amanda's hand so that she can sign her name. That's when Polly turns to look, so she can always remember Amanda as she is right now, straining to sign over everything she owns, still finding something worth giving.

Charlie and Al and Claire stand in the front yard for a long time. Across the street there are still pumpkins on the porches and black cats taped to the windows. After she'd been carried into the Blazer, Amanda looked out her window and waved to them. Charlie can't stop remembering that, the way her hand moved like a piece of white paper.

"It's cold out here," Claire says.

"You're right," Al agrees.

They start for the house, then stop.

"Charlie?" Al says.

"I'm not going in there," Charlie says. He's still looking at the place in the driveway where the Blazer was parked.

"Charlie," Claire says.

"Let him be," Al tells her.

Charlie stands on the lawn while his grandparents go inside. In a little while the door opens again and Charlie winces. He doesn't want to talk to anyone, but it's not his grandmother, it's just Al. Al comes up behind him and stands out there with him.

"Amanda left something for you," Al says. When Charlie doesn't answer Al asks, "Did you hear me?"

"I heard you," Charlie says.

"I think she'd want you to have it now."

Charlie faces Al, and when he sees his sister's gym bag he takes it and walks into the house. He goes down to the basement and gets the Minolta, the light meter, the flash, and a new box of film, puts them all into the gym bag, then goes back upstairs.

"I know what we'll do," his grandmother says when she sees him. "We'll play canasta."

"I'm going to go for a ride," Charlie says.

"Does your mother allow you to do that?" Claire asks, worried.

"Of course she does," Al says. "Give the boy a break."

"I want you back here in one hour," Claire tells Charlie. "Don't stay out any later than that."

Al squeezes Charlie's shoulder, then lets him go. Charlie runs out to his bike, gets on, and pedals as hard as he can. He rides for a long time. He goes past the marsh, and out on the road to the beach where he's not allowed to go. The salt air here makes his eyes sting; it hurts his lungs when he breathes too deeply. He goes farther than he's ever gone alone. By the time he circles around to the pond, more than an hour has passed.

His grandmother is probably going crazy, but he doesn't care. The path he follows is covered with wet leaves; last night's rain has made the path slick, it's dangerous for bike riding, but Charlie just goes faster. This is the time of year when it's easy to see deer. The time, too, when there are likely to be fresh bullet holes in the DEER CROSSING signs.

Charlie gets off his bike and crouches down next to it. No matter what, there will always be two kids in their family. Even if everything she owned is thrown away, even if her closets are empty, her room will always belong to her, and whenever he's asked, at school or by a stranger he meets, he'll always say, "I have one sister, Amanda," because he always will. He'll have her long after his parents have grown old and died, and if he ever has children of his own he'll tell them everything about her, what her favorite music was, the names she used to call him, everything, so they'll remember her, too.

He sits there by his bike for more than an hour. He doesn't care what his grandparents think, he's not going home. When he finally gets up to walk closer to the pond, his sneakers sink into the mud. He carries his camera equipment in the gym bag and he sits down. He doesn't care if his jeans get all muddy, but he's careful with the gym bag and puts it down on some pine needles. There is a lone dragonfly with blue wings skittering over the water. A fat green frog, who will soon disappear for the winter when the pond begins to freeze over, sits in the last of the sunlight. Something larger than a frog is moving in the center of the pond, and Charlie quietly edges closer. He opens the gym bag with one hand, lifts out the Minolta, and holds it to his eye. He hears a swishing noise and a moment passes before what it is registers: it's the sound of a bike riding on damp leaves. Charlie lets the camera down and turns to see Sevrin dropping his bike down. Charlie quickly turns back to the pond

217

and raises his camera again. Whatever had been moving is motionless now.

"Your grandmother's calling your friends to find you," Sevrin says. "I figured you'd be here."

"Brilliant deduction," Charlie says.

"Yeah," Sevrin says with a laugh. "What are you photographing?"

Sevrin walks a little closer to the pond and almost loses his balance on the slick leaves.

"Does your mother know you're here?" Charlie says.

"No," Sevrin says defensively. "And neither does yours. Or your grandmother, either."

"That's different," Charlie says.

Sevrin sits down a few feet away.

"The kids in my new school are assholes," Sevrin says. "One kid brings his homework to school in an attaché case. I swear to God."

"Oh, yeah?" Charlie says.

He focuses on the center of the pond. If Amanda were here she'd probably want to go swimming. Cold water never bothered her. It's getting dark fast and Charlie reaches into the gym bag for the light meter.

"That's Amanda's," Sevrin says.

Charlie turns to Sevrin and glares at him. "What if it is?" he says, daring Sevrin to say something nasty about the gym bag because it's pink.

"Neat dinosaur patch," Sevrin says.

Charlie turns back and refocuses. He recognizes the sound of Sevrin tapping his foot. Sevrin always does that when he's nervous.

"Look, I don't care if you hate me," Sevrin says. "You're still my best friend."

Through the camera, things look more yellow than they are.

218

Shadows seem darker, more permanent. Charlie will never let himself forget her. Not in a million years.

"Hand me the flash," Charlie says.

Sevrin scurries over to the gym bag and gets the flash attachment for him.

"Maybe you'd better go home," Charlie says. "Your mother's going to be worried about you. You'll just be wasting your time. I haven't even seen that turtle since the last time we were here."

Sevrin thinks this over carefully. "That's okay," he says. "If anyone sees him, it'll be us."

There are many national and local organizations working to combat AIDS, among them the American Foundation for AIDS Research. Donations, made out to AMFAR, may be sent to:

At Risk
American Foundation for AIDS Research
40 West 57th Street
Suite 406
New York, New York 10019